Tales from Devana High

Jugglin'

Also in this series:

Concrete Chips
Sold as Seen
What's Up?

Tales from Devana High

Jugglin'

Bali Rai

A division of Hodder Headline Limited

First published in 2006 by
Hodder Children's Books

1

A Catalogue record for this book is available from
the British Library

ISBN 0 340 87731 6

Typeset in Garamond by Avon DataSet Ltd,
Bidford-on-Avon, Warwickshire

Printed and bound in Great Britain by
Bookmarque Ltd, Croydon, Surrey

The paper and board used in this paperback are natural recyclable
products made from wood grown in sustainable forests.
The manufacturing processes conform to the environmental
regulations of the country of origin.

Hodder Children's Books
A division of Hodder Headline Limited
338 Euston Road
London NW1 3BH

To Class 7HO at Ripley St Thomas School
in Lancaster for dreaming up Andy Stevenson;
and to class 7L6 at Oakbank School
(and Miss Angel) in Keighley for
Matt Dwibble . . . nice one!

ONE

'Suky!'

I opened my bedroom door and called down to my mum. 'I'm up!'

'Well come downstairs then,' she replied.

I checked my hair in the mirror one more time, grabbed my school bag and went downstairs to the kitchen, where my mum and dad were eating toast. My dad wiped crumbs from his mouth before speaking to me, the dirty old git.

'You want a lift?' he said.

I grabbed a slice of toast as I replied, 'Please . . .'

My dad grinned. I knew there was something else coming. Something that only he would think was funny.

'Want to pick up the boyfriend on the way?' he teased.

'Er . . . no – he makes his own way to school,' I told him.

I was talking about *both* of my boyfriends. My real one, Imtiaz and my fake one, Jit. My parents had only met Jit and that was who my dad was on about. I put some jam on my toast and started to eat, hoping that my dad would lay off. As I finished it my grandma walked into the kitchen holding her false teeth.

'Aren't you going to get dressed?' she mumbled in Punjabi, looking at me.

'I'm *already* dressed,' I pointed out.

'Stupid cow,' replied my grandma.

I suppose I should explain a few things really. First off, my grandma is completely senile so no one batted an eyelid when she called me a stupid cow. Secondly, there's a good reason why I've got 'two' boyfriends. My real boyfriend is called Imtiaz. He's in my class at school and I've known him since infant school. But he's Muslim and my parents are Sikhs and I thought they might have a problem with him even though they know Imi – they've met him and his parents loads of times. My parents started asking me to bring my boyfriend home so that they could meet him and I kind of lied and told them I was seeing a lad called Jit, who is Sikh, and in my class at school. They met Jit and liked him and now I'm stuck. It's a delicate situation and one of these days I'm going to have to tell them the truth, but not yet.

My dad, whose name is Randeep, zipped his tracksuit top up over his beer belly and told me to hurry up.

'I'm ready' I replied.

'And, by the way,' added my mum, who's called Tina, 'we're planning a family day trip to the seaside soon. You can ask Jit along if you like . . .'

I swallowed hard. Would Jit go for that? He'd already helped me out enough, coming along to various family events, only to get a grilling from my Uncle Mandeep and my dad; and to get sworn at by the mad witch who was masquerading as my grandmother.

'Er . . . I'll see what he says,' I replied.

My grandma farted.

'That son of a *dung* collector?' she said, to no one in particular. 'Tell him we don't want his kind in this house. He's so ugly I cry every time I see him . . .'

I gave her a dirty look before getting up from the table.

'Just ignore her,' my mum advised.

'Have you cleaned your teeth, you witch?' added my gran, looking at my mum.

My dad shook his head and started giggling like a little boy.

'Don't encourage her,' my mum hissed.

'She don't need any encouragement,' he replied. 'Mad as a pregnant water buffalo, that one . . .'

I grinned at my dad.

'Come on then,' he said. 'Let's get you to school so that you can play kissing games with Jit . . .'

'Dad!'

I got out of my dad's car at the school gates. My school is called Devana High, which is a stupid name for a school if you ask me, but it's kind of a cool place. The principal, Mr Black, was standing at the school gates as usual, watching the pupils arrive.

'Early again, Miss Kaur,' he bellowed at me in his foghorn voice.

'Yessir,' I mumbled, hoping that he'd leave me alone.

'We should present you with an award for your timekeeping,' he added, beaming a wide smile in my direction, just as another one of my classmates, Hannah, turned up.

'Er . . . yes Sir,' I said, feeling embarrassed.

'Ooh nerdy bum lick,' whispered Hannah, before giggling.

'Shut up,' I told her, as we walked into school through the main entrance.

'Well – you and your nice relationship with Black – you're a creep.'

'But you're always on time too,' I reminded her, 'so what does that make you?'

'Diligent and punctual,' she replied. 'But neither of those things involves being a bum lick . . .'

'Oh, get lost . . .'

We walked into our form room and took our usual seats. Imtiaz (my *real* boyfriend) was already there and he smiled at me as I sat down.

'Hi,' I said.

'You all right?' he asked me.

'Yeah – why wouldn't I be?' I replied.

'It's just that you said you were going to call me yesterday and you didn't,' he told me, looking like a little boy.

'Sorry . . . forgot,' I replied, feeling a bit guilty.

'How can you *forget* to call your boyfriend?' asked Hannah, before grinning. 'Oh *yeah* – you've got *two* . . .'

I looked at Imi whose face fell.

'I've only got one *real* boyfriend,' I corrected. 'Jit's just like a stand-in . . .'

'You spend enough time with him, though,' added Hannah.

I glared at her. Didn't she get it? I didn't want her to wind up Imi by talking about Jit. Talk about upsetting the applecart. I think she got my meaning because she went red.

'So, you just forgot?' continued Imi.

'Er . . . yeah. I was with my mum and dad and didn't get a chance and . . .'

'It doesn't matter,' he added.

I grinned at him. Behind us our form tutor, Mrs Dooher walked in.

'Morning!' she said in her lovely Liverpudlian accent.

'Hi Miss!' beamed Hannah.

'And you call *me* a bum lick?' I said.

'Oh shut up – Mrs Dooher is lovely.'

'So is Mr Black,' I pointed out.

'Is what, Suky?' asked Mrs Dooher from behind me.

'A nice man,' I said quickly.

'And you're talking about him because . . .?' she continued.

'We're just comparing teachers, Miss,' said Hannah, winking at me. 'You know – who we really like and who we don't. You came top of the list . . .'

Mrs Dooher smiled warily.

'Soft gits . . .' she said, before turning her attention to Marco and Milorad, twin brothers who were having a scuffle.

'STOP IT!' she half-shouted.

'But he called me a toad licker!' squealed Marco.

'Didn't!' replied his twin brother.

'Why a toad licker?' asked Mrs Dooher, as Jit, Dean

and Grace walked in, two minutes before time.

'Who's lickin' toads, Miss?' asked Dean.

'No one,' I told him. 'The ugly twins are having a scrap, that's all . . .'

'Who you callin' ugly?' shouted Marco. 'Have you seen a mirror lately . . .'

I felt myself go red, but Jit stepped in.

'You'll be ugly when I've finished with you,' he told Marco.

'Uglier than your brother,' added Dean, 'and my guy is butt ugly, you get me? I seen better looking warts than him . . .'

Mrs Dooher sighed and told us all to sit down.

'But why a toad licker?' asked Grace. 'That's just dirty . . .'

'You *can* lick toads though,' said Dean.

'HUH?' asked Hannah.

'Yeah – they got 'em in South America. They lick them and get all high and that – except for one yellow one though. If you licked *that* toad you'd be dead . . .'

'But why would anyone *want* to lick a toad – stinky, smelly . . .' continued Grace, only I switched off because Jit asked me if I was OK.

'Yes – how about you?'

'All right,' he told me. 'Them twins won't be picking on you again . . .'

I gave him a big smile; only Imi saw me do it and I could tell by the look on his face that he was throwing a wobbly. So I gave *him* an even bigger smile but it was too late. Imi looked away and started talking to a lad called Dilip instead.

TWO

I wanted to ask him about my family trip to the seaside although I couldn't be sure that he would agree to come along. He'd already been to a few family events and our 'little blag' as he called it wasn't supposed to have been a long-term thing. I was *supposed* to find a way of telling my parents about Imi gently – you know, test the water first – but it was just too easy to pretend that Jit was my boyfriend. Plus, I had cold feet about telling my parents the truth anyway, so I was happy for things to continue as they were. The problem was that Jit was expecting the opposite, as was Imi. And then there was Grace, who pretended that she didn't fancy Jit but had been funny with us both since our 'blag' had begun.

I was walking into English with Hannah, Imi and Grace when I saw Jit. Imi saw him too and when I took Jit to one side, Imi frowned at me. I waited for him to go into the classroom before I spoke. I could always talk him round later.

'I need another favour,' I blurted out.

Jit shrugged.

'What this time?' he asked.

'Family day out . . . to the seaside,' I told him.

'Suky . . .'

'I know I said the other week would be the last time but my dad just dropped this on me . . .'

'I dunno,' he told me. 'We're gonna get caught out one day . . . why don't you just tell your dad the truth . . .'

I shrugged.

'I'm going to – soon, I promise. It's just that he really likes you and . . .'

'But that just makes it worse,' he told me. 'The more he gets used to the idea that you an' me are seein' each other – the harder it's going to be to tell him about Imi.'

'Just one more time . . . please?' I begged.

'I dunno, Suky. I'm not into all this jugglin' business . . .'

'Jugglin'?'

'Yeah – you know. Like the way you're jugglin' two lads an' that . . .'

'Oh right . . . *Jugglin'* – I like it . . . so will you think about it at least?' I asked.

'Yeah, OK. But I'm not sitting in a car with your gran

– she called me a one-legged son of a vulture the other week . . .'

'I thought that you couldn't speak Punjabi that well . . .?' I said, grinning.

'I can't – your old man told me what she was on about and then he laughed at me for ages . . .'

'I'm *sorry*,' I said, in a girly voice, feeling a bit guilty because it was the voice I used when I was flirting with Imi.

'I'll tell you whether I can help later,' Jit said.

'GET INTO THE CLASSROOM!' shouted our English teacher, Mr Herbert.

'Yeah, yeah,' sighed Jit, walking over to Dean and sitting down. I walked past them and sat down by Imi. Dilip and another boy, Mohammed, whistled as I took my chair.

'QUIET!' squawked Herbert, going red in the face.

'Kiss my fat raas,' muttered Dean.

Herbert's head snapped round so fast that I thought it would come off.

'WHAT DID YOU SAY?' he demanded.

Dean grinned. 'I said that school discipline is a farce,' he lied. 'A big *fat* farce . . .'

'Well keep it to yourself,' warned Herbert.

'If I was as ugly as you, I would,' muttered Jit.

'WHAT?'

'I *said* that it doesn't take much to be good,' lied Jit. 'In school, I mean . . .'

'And you're the expert, are you?' sneered Herbert. The red mark on his forehead, where he'd squeezed a giant pimple a few days earlier, turned a darker shade. I smiled at the memory of seeing him walk back into the room with a load of blood where his spot used to be. It had been one of the funniest things that I had ever seen.

At lunchtime I was sitting in a classroom with Hannah and Grace working on the school newspaper when Imi walked in looking like someone had slapped his face with a dead fish.

'What's up with you?' asked Grace. 'You look ill . . .'

'Nothing,' he replied, pulling up a chair. 'What you doin'?'

I showed him some magazine articles on chat-up lines.

'We're doing a feature on rubbish boys and what they say to try and pull girls,' Hannah told him.

'Yeah – like "did you fall out of Heaven . . ." and other silly stuff,' added Grace.

'Oh,' replied Imi.

'What's up?' This time I was asking.

Imi shrugged. 'Just feeling a bit under the weather,' he told me.

He was lying. I knew what was up with him, and I told him that we needed to talk. Hannah and Grace both raised their eyebrows, like they were twins. I scowled at them and walked into the corridor, behind Imi. I didn't say anything until the door was firmly closed and the twins couldn't hear what we were saying.

'It's about Jit isn't it?' I said to Imi.

'NO!'

'Yes, it is . . .'

He shrugged.

'You just seem to be spending a load of time with him,' he said. 'You may as well be going out with him.'

'But I'm not,' I told him. 'I'm going out with you . . .'

'Yeah . . .'

'Yeah – nothing. All this stuff with Jit is just to fool my parents. It's not *real* . . .' I interrupted.

'May as well be *real*,' he sulked.

'Imi!'

'He was even standing up for you this morning with Marco. He's never done that before.'

'Yes he has – and anyway we're much better friends than we used to be. He's cool . . .'

Imi looked down at his feet as I realised my mistake. I'd put my foot in it.

'Oh you *know* what I mean,' I insisted. 'I'm just jugglin' – that's all. Not because I want to but . . .'

'*See?* You're even beginning to talk like him. Since when did you use words like *that?*'

'Like what?'

'Jugglin' . . . what's that all about?'

I shook my head. Imi was beginning to wind me up. I really liked him and I could understand why he was bothered but there was a limit.

'It's only a *word*,' I said.

'No – it's a *Jit* word,' he replied. Then he walked off.

'*IMI*!' I shouted after him but he didn't reply.

I swore under my breath and went back into the classroom, pushing the door open to find Grace and Hannah behind it.

'Oh, great!' I said, stomping over to my chair.

Hannah grinned at me but Grace gave me a funny look.

'What?' I asked her.

'Was that about Jit?'

I nodded.

'Do you like *him* too?' she added.

'Yeah, but not like *that*. Jit's really cool. I used to think he was nuts but he can be really quite mature and clever and . . .'

I saw Grace pull a similar face to Imi.

'I told you – it's not like that!' I shouted.

'Easy now . . .' Hannah told me.

'I don't care, anyway,' said Grace, lying through her teeth. I knew she fancied Jit. Everyone did. And Jit fancied her too. The only people who couldn't work it out were Grace and Jit.

'Yes you do . . . but you've got it all wrong . . .'

Grace pretended to yawn.

'I'm bored now,' she told us. 'I'm going to go and find the lads . . .'

Then she walked out too. 'That's just great!' I told Hannah.

'I'm not saying anything . . .' she replied, although I could see that she wanted to.

THREE

When I got home my dad was in the kitchen, making himself a sandwich with about three different cold meats.

'Isn't that pastrami?' I asked him as he loaded up a slice of thickly buttered bread.

'Yeah . . . I've never tried it before . . .'

'And chicken and ham?'

'So?'

'On buttered bread. With mayonnaise . . .?'

My dad grinned at me. 'I'm hungry . . .'

'But you're not supposed to have butter. It's bad for you. And pastrami is made from beef, you know.'

My dad picked up a slice of the offending meat and stuffed it into his mouth.

'Tastes good though,' he told me, spitting bits of it everywhere.

'Dad!'

He ignored me, and smeared a big dollop of mayo on

the other slice before pushing it down to finish his sandwich.

'I thought Sikhs didn't eat beef?' I pointed out.

'Well . . . it's not like I'm a proper Sikh anyway. I'm sure one bit of beef won't send me to Hell. And what about those cheeseburgers you eat . . .?'

'You bought me those.'

He grinned. 'Oh yeah.'

As he stood at the counter and ate his food I wondered about what he'd said about not being a proper Sikh. Did that mean he wouldn't mind me seeing Imi? I wanted to ask him about it but my mobile phone went off just as I was working up the courage. I looked at the screen to see Imi's name flashing next to a little bunch of flowers.

'That the boyfriend?' mumbled my dad through another big mouthful of food.

'Suppose so,' I said, walking over to the kitchen door and out into the garden.

Our garden is quite big and I walked all the way down to the end of it, through some trees into a hidden bit at the back talking to Imi. I arranged to meet him by some shops, which were around the corner from Grace's house. When I got back to the house my dad was just about to leave.

'I'm going back to the factory,' he told me, talking about one of the businesses that he ran with my mum. They also owned a cash and carry warehouse, three launderettes, about five houses that they rented out and a Punjabi clothing shop. I asked him where my mum was.

'Dunno . . . she's had to wait for a delivery at the cash and carry. Should be back in about half an hour.'

'I'm goin' out anyway,' I replied. 'But if you speak to her, tell her I'll be back about seven . . .'

'Yes, *Madam*,' he told me.

Imi was standing outside the sports shop where my dad had bought me all of my gear over the years. I love sport and I'm kind of good at it. I pick things up really quickly too. At the moment I'm obsessed with badminton and football and I know that I'll be better than the lads soon. Even Dean, and he's almost as sporty as I am – although I always beat him at sprinting.

'Hi,' I said, as I walked up to my boyfriend.

'Hi.'

His voice was kind of flat but I didn't let it put me off. I was going to cheer him up whether he liked it or not. I gave him a kiss on the cheek.

'You OK now?' I asked, as he went a bit red. He nodded.

'I'm fine, now . . . sorry about before. I was acting like an idiot,' he admitted.

'Don't worry about it,' I said.

'So what do you want to do then?'

'Normal stuff . . . cinema maybe.'

He grinned. 'There's this great film on . . .'

'Well, let me call my mum and tell her I won't be in until even later,' I replied.

When I'd finished not answering my mum's questions about where I was going and all that stuff, I grabbed Imi's hand and we walked to a bus stop, one that was a long way from my parents' house.

Imi walked me halfway home before setting off for his own. We had a little set route that we took whenever we were in our own area which involved us almost zigzagging our way through the streets before ending up near Grace's house. Then I went left and Imi went right. I didn't like having to sneak around but I hadn't plucked up the courage to tell my parents abut Imi; and he hadn't told his parents about me either. When I got in I thought about telling my mum there and then only I bumped into my mental gran first.

'Where have you been? Don't you know that young

girls shouldn't be out on their own? People will talk . . .' she spat at me in Punjabi.

'But I've been to my friend's house,' I replied.

'In my day . . .' she began, and went to find my mum. She was in the kitchen sitting with a cup of herbal tea, staring into space.

'What you doing – meditating?' I asked her.

'Not really,' she said, not looking up.

'Trouble at work?' I asked.

'Trouble full stop,' she replied.

My heart sank for a second as I worried that she had found out about me and Imtiaz but it was something that was even more shocking.

'Mum?'

'I'm pregnant,' she replied, looking at me for the first time.

'What?'

'I'm pregnant . . . you know . . .?'

'EURRGH!'

'Oh, don't be so silly,' she snapped.

'I just don't want to know about the details . . . that's disgusting!'

My mum stood up and took my hands in hers.

'Aren't you excited . . . you're going to have a little brother or sister,' she said.

'Are *you* excited?' I asked in reply. 'You don't look it.'

She smiled and gave me a hug. 'Of course I am – It's just a bit of a shock . . .'

'You didn't plan it?'

She shrugged. 'Not really . . . we just kind of . . .'

'NO WAY! I don't want to know at all. I'm really happy and all of that stuff but please . . . dirty old people . . .'

She pinched my cheeks like she used to when I was a baby. Only it didn't hurt then because they were chubby. They weren't chubby any more though and it really did hurt but I kept a straight face.

'You'd better start thinking up some names,' she told me.

God – you think you *know* your parents and then they go and hit you with a brick.

FOUR

'Paulo?' suggested Hannah the next day at school.

'What?' I asked wondering what she was on about.

'*Names* . . . for your baby brother or sister? You did ask me for some . . .'

I shrugged. 'Oh yeah . . .'

'You freak. You only asked me like minus twenty million seconds ago . . .' she continued.

'Sorry, I was thinking about something else,' I told her.

'Your boyfriends . . .?'

'Kind of. I want to tell my mum the truth about Imi but I don't know where to begin.'

'How about telling her that you mistakenly assumed she was prejudiced and so you've been telling her brazen, bare-faced lies ever since. Would that work?' she joked.

'Possibly not, Miss Meadows but thanks for nothing . . .'

'Oh, why not just tell her you were scared . . .' Hannah suggested.

'Scared of what?'

'Anything,' she replied. 'When I was little and I did something naughty and I got caught I used to pretend to my mum I was scared. I used to just make up what I was scared of and every time she felt sorry for me and forgot to tell me off.'

'Don't think that'll do it either,' I sighed.

'Worked for me.'

We were sitting on a radiator in the main corridor watching other pupils walk past. I hadn't seen Jit at all and was just wondering where he was when two lads from our year, Robert and Wesley, came over and grinned at us like lunatics.

'Something to say, Mr Magoogan?' Hannah asked Wesley.

'You could say that . . .' replied Wesley, his smile widening even further. I didn't think people could open their mouths that wide.

'Are you going to tell us what it is?' continued Hannah. 'Or am I going to have to snog it out of Mr Sargeant?'

She was talking about Robert who lost his smile for a moment, went red, and stammered, 'Um . . . um . . . er . . .' he said, as Hannah winked at me.

'Spit it out, there's a good boy,' I said to him.

Wesley saved his friend from more embarrassment. 'We've been selected to play in a chess challenge for the school,' he told us.

Hannah groaned. 'Is that all? I thought you had something *really* interesting to tell us . . .' she moaned.

'It is . . .' added Robert, after he'd calmed down. 'It's a national challenge, held in Birmingham. Timed games against the best in the country. We're really very privileged.'

'And you're telling us because we've just spent the last year in isolation and find even the most mind-numbingly boring things interesting, I suppose?' I replied.

'Er . . .'

'Mr Black would like you to cover our selection and future progress in your little newspaper,' said Wesley.

'Oh, great!' said Hannah.

'That's what we thought,' replied Robert, thinking that he was agreeing with her but failing to notice the heavy edge of sarcasm in her voice. Typical boy.

'No,' explained Hannah, 'I didn't mean great as in *good* – I meant . . .'

'We'd love to,' I interrupted. 'Anything for the good of the school.'

'That's what we thought,' agreed Wesley.

'Still reading that fantasy series?' asked Hannah. '*The Dark Lord of Whatever . .?*'

Robert and Wesley both beamed at the same time. 'It's wonderful . . .' said Wesley.

'But we're waiting for the sequels to be published,' added Robert.

'Although that *does* give us an opportunity to re-read the other books,' finished Wesley.

'Sequels?' I asked.

'There's gonna be two of them,' I heard Dean say from behind me.

'Hi, Dean!'

'Yeah . . . two more and then two more and eventually the whole of every bookshop and library is gonna be full of only those books . . .'

'Heaven,' sighed Robert.

'If that's as good as your idea of Heaven gets, you is in big trouble, you get me?' replied Dean, winking at me.

'But . . . I . . . er . . .' stammered Robert for the second time in five minutes.

'I mean, I'm thinking 'bout cars and gal and diamonds and ting and there's you wit' a million books about the same messed-up fantasy world . . .' continued Dean.

'Well *we* like them,' said Wesley.

And with that he grabbed Robert and they walked off.

'What about your article?' Hannah shouted after them but they didn't reply.

'Cheers, Dean,' I said. 'Now we're going to have to be nice to them.'

'Just flash a bit of leg,' he told me.

I punched him on the arm. 'OWW!'

'Oh, don't be such a girl!' laughed Hannah.

'If he was a girl he wouldn't have screamed. He's a little boy,' I told her.

'Kiss my . . .' he began only he didn't finish.

Someone shouted, and them someone else screamed and Jit came running past us as fast he could. Behind him an older lad, who looked like he was half skunk, was chasing; and behind him was Jason Patel.

'What the . . .' shouted Dean, as he set off after Jit and the two older lads.

I looked at Hannah. 'I thought Jason Patel had been kicked out of school?' I asked.

'So did I?'

Two teachers went running past us too as I replied.

'So, what is he doing back at school . . .?'

'Dunno,' said Hannah, jumping off the radiator, 'but I'm going to find out.'

I groaned and then followed her as she followed the rest.

We didn't find them though. We walked all the way around the school but they had disappeared. And then it was time for our next lesson. Jit and Dean didn't show up for that either, but the maths teacher, Mrs Lee-Cross didn't even mention it. She was obviously aware of what was going on. Grace looked worried and, after the lesson, I asked her what had happened.

'Jit was talking to me when Jason Patel appeared out of nowhere and punched him,' she told me.

'Oh my God!' I replied, really concerned.

Grace gave me a funny look and then continued.

'He was with some other lad – the one with the funny hair and Jit ran off. They went after him . . .'

'But I thought that Jason had been kicked out?'

Grace shrugged. 'He's obviously come back for some reason . . .'

'Well, I'm gonna go and see Jit after school' I said. 'Make sure he's OK.'

'You don't need to do that' Grace snapped. 'I'll do it. He was my friend first . . .'

'Grace that's just being silly . . .'

'I don't care,' she replied. 'Since you started lying to your parents I've hardly seen him. You don't have a special Jit-only licence . . .'

'But . . .' I began, realising that she was really upset with me.

'Oh forget it,' she snapped again. 'I'm off to art . . .'

I tried to speak to her all the way through our last lesson but she just ignored me and carried on painting. After school I went to the loo and when I got back to Hannah, Grace had gone.

'Her mum picked her up,' Hannah told me.

'I should call her – she's pissed off with me . . .'

Hannah shrugged. 'If I was you I'd leave it for a while. You know what she's like about Jit . . .'

'Yeah but I'm not trying to take Jit away . . . we've just got quite close in the last few weeks, that's all . . .'

Once again my timing was rubbish. Just as I'd finished my last sentence, Imtiaz appeared next to me.

'Talking about your boyfriend, again?' he asked.

'Oh don't be so silly – we were only—' I began.

'I couldn't care less,' he whined before he walked off too.

'This is getting silly now,' I told Hannah.

'Yep . . . sillier than a sun hat for cows . . .'

'Huh . . .'

But she didn't explain. Instead she headed off out of school, past two year sevens who were pulling a rabbit along the corridor on a dog leash.

'What *exactly* are you doing?' I asked them.

'Mind your own business,' squealed one of them.

'You lanky witch . . .' said the other.

'Charming' I replied, storming off after Hannah.

FIVE

The next day I found out what was going on. I was in registration with Imi, who had calmed down, and Grace, who refused to tell me anything about what had happened to Jit and Dean.

'If you're so close to Jit, why hasn't he told you himself?' she sneered, like a little girl.

'You irritating little witch!' I replied.

'Oh, yeah – cos she's really gonna tell you if you call her names,' Hannah pointed out.

'I'm sorry, Grace,' I said.

Grace had been my friend since we'd met at infant school but she was a bit of a freak. Sometimes she'd be happy as anything and talking about silly stuff and the next she'd get all arsey and behave like we were still infants. I knew she was upset so I let it go, hoping that I could make her see sense eventually. I didn't want to lose my oldest friend over a misunderstanding.

'Smelly bum,' she replied, making me want to strangle her all over again.

Eventually Mrs Dooher walked in with a really young looking, skinny lad in tow. He was blond with mad frizzy hair that stuck out at all different angles. I asked Imi who it was.

'I dunno – new kid?'

I looked back at the lad. His ears looked as though they were lop-sided and his glasses were too big for his face; and he had goofy teeth. I could see that the lads in class were going to have fun teasing him and I started to feel sorry for him before it had even happened. But my sympathy didn't last long.

'Suky?' said Mrs Dooher.

'Yes, Miss?'

'This is Matthew . . . Matt Dribble . . . he's new,' she began.

'Not surprised he dribbles with teeth like that,' shouted Milorad.

'Be quiet!' warned Mrs Dooher.

'But Miss . . .' complained Milorad.

'Oh, go away!' Mrs Dooher half-shouted, looking flustered.

'Do you want me to show him round?' I asked.

'Yes . . . you, and Jit – when he eventually arrives.'

I didn't want to, but I looked at Grace. It wasn't one of those looks that says 'haha – I get to be with the boy you fancy' but she took it that way, going red and turning her head. I tried to salvage the situation.

'But can't me and Imi do it . . .?'

'You already are – doing it, innit?' shouted Dilip.

'Oh shut up you immature little bed-wetter,' I told him.

'Oooooh!' said half the class.

'Bumpin' uglies!' shouted Raj, another lad.

'Calm down . . .' warned Mrs Dooher again, in her own, quiet, rubbish sort of way.

'So, can we?' I repeated. 'Only Jit isn't here yet . . .'

'Yes I am!' said Jit, as he walked in with Dean in tow.

Mrs Dooher gave them a big smile even though they were nearly late.

'What do you want me to do, Miss?' he asked.

'Show our new boy, Matt, around. With Suky,' she told him.

Grace mumbled something under her breath but I ignored it.

'I don't mind,' said Jit. Then he saw Matt and his jaw fell open and he turned to Dean.

'Don't look at me, bro,' Dean told him. 'You is the one that offered . . .'

'You can both start your first lesson ten minutes late . . . I've cleared it. I want you to show him all around the school but be quick. And then can you let him hang around with you over break and lunch?'

'S'pose . . .' mumbled Jit, coming over to join the rest of us, as Hannah ran into the room.

'Sorry I'm late, Miss,' she squirmed.

'Don't do it again,' said Mrs Dooher. See? Rubbish at discipline. Which is why we all loved her so much.

'What happened with Jason Patel?' asked Imi, as Dean and Jit sat down.

'It wasn't Jason,' Dean told us, as even Grace turned round to hear.

'Yes it was . . . we all saw him,' I replied.

Dean shook his head.

'It's even worse,' he said. 'That ugly bwoi you seen yesterday was *Justin* Patel – Jason's cousin . . .'

'What?'

'It's no lie,' said Jit. 'And he's brought an even uglier friend this time – Andy Stevenson.'

'The boy with hair that looked like a skunk's arse?' asked Hannah.

'Yeah – him . . .' growled Jit.

'But why are they after you two?' said Imi.

'Revenge,' explained Dean. 'We're in the shit, big time, you get me?'

'That's just silly,' I told him. 'Mr Black won't put up with people from outside coming in and causing trouble . . .'

'That's just it, Suky,' added Jit, as Grace pulled another face. 'They's new pupils . . . them man are part of the school.'

As if right on cue, Matt walked over to us and sat in the only available chair.

'Hello!' said Hannah, smiling at him.

'Hi . . .' said Matt, in a high-pitched voice.

'Where are you from then?'

Matt shrugged and said nothing.

'*Well*?' asked Dean. 'Cos if you wanna sit with the cool people you need to get with the programme, you get me?'

'Oh,' said Matt. 'I think I get you . . .'

When he opened his mouth to speak I saw that two of his teeth were dark yellow and that he had bits of food stuck between them. I cringed.

'So, let's start again,' said Dean. 'How you doin' Matty, my man?'

'I'm fine,' he replied.

'And which part of this fair city have you come from . . .?'

'Round Belgrave way . . .' he told us.

'An' what—?' began Dean, only for Mrs Dooher to tell him to shut up.

'But I'm just bein' nice, Miss . . .' he complained.

I saw Dilip and Mohammed smirk and waited for them to tease someone. 'Suky's always nice, Miss. Maybe Dribble-pants can be her third boyfriend?'

They giggled and Matt went red.

'I'm gonna stick that pen you're holding up your nose in a minute,' warned Jit.

'Try it!' challenged Dilip, in his whiny voice. 'I'll tell Miss—'

Jit pushed back his chair and Dilip flinched.

'See how you jump,' laughed Dean. 'Knobhead . . .'

'*Miss*!' squealed Dilip.

Mrs Dooher sighed, told us to shut up again and took the register.

Jit showed Matt where the boys' toilets were after registration because he was dying to use the loo.

'I've got a bladder problem,' he told us.

Jit grinned at me as we waited for him in the corridor.

'That bwoi is unfortunate,' he told me.

'Jit – that's not fair . . . he's new . . .' I said.

'And funny looking . . .'

'Don't be mean,' I said, before asking him some more about Justin Patel and Andy Stevenson.

'They told me that they were going to make my life a misery,' grinned Jit. 'Like I ain't had that already . . .'

He was talking about the trouble he'd had with his mum's last boyfriend, Micky who had been a bully. But Jit had come up with a plan to get rid of him and it had worked.

'You need to be careful though,' I told him. 'They might hurt you . . .'

I put my hand on his arm and then, realising that I'd done it I pulled away. Jit gave me a funny look and then looked away.

'They ain't nuttin',' he told me. 'I can handle them . . .'

'Ooh macho boy,' I grinned.

'You mean, man?' he corrected.

'Uh-uh – I mean boy,' I replied.

'Cheeky cow . . .!'

'Oi!'

I pushed him playfully into the wall, which is when my bad luck with timing came back and hit me on the head. Jit grabbed my arm as I pushed him and I kind of fell into him, just as the door to the girls' toilets opened and Puspha, a girl in our form walked out. She looked at us, grinned and then started to giggle.

'Wait till I tell everyone else!' she said.

'But it's not what you think . . .' I protested.

'Yeah, yeah,' she said, walking back to her lesson.

'But . . .'

Jit let go of my arm.

'Don't worry about it,' he told me. 'We were just messing about . . .'

I shrugged.

'That's not how she's gonna tell it,' I said.

Jit shrugged too.

'Who cares?' he said.

In my head I went through a list of names. Grace, Imi, my parents, but I didn't say anything out loud.

'What the hell is he doing in there?' asked Jit.

'Er . . . it's a loo. What do people usually do in the loo?' I replied. 'No, second thoughts – scratch that. I don't wanna think about it.'

'I'm going to make sure he ain't fallen down the plug hole,' said Jit. 'Seeing as how he's that skinny . . .'

I watched him walk in and after a few seconds heard a loud braying, like a donkey on laughing gas. Then Jit walked out into the corridor.

'Man – you hear that laugh?' he asked me.

'Yeah – is that Matt?'

Jit nodded. 'I told him to hurry up or we might bump into Santa Claus and he did *that* . . .'

'What – laughed?'

'If that's what you'd call it,' he said.

The toilet door opened and Matt walked out.

'That wewey was a vewy funny joke,' he said, as I realised that he had a speech thing. He couldn't pronounce 'r' properly. I hadn't noticed it in class earlier on but it was very pronounced. Or Pwonounced even . . .

'Yes it was,' grinned Jit, sensing the chance to make fun of Matt. 'Wewey, Wewey funny. Mr Dwibbler has got a sense of humour . . .'

I shook my head and punched Jit on the arm again. The idiot.

SIX

The following Saturday morning I had to get up early and go shopping with my dad. We went to our local Asda and I spent the most of the time there avoiding bumping into people. It was packed and everyone in there was annoying me, including my dad, who was going around picking up things that weren't on the shopping list.

'Never tried this,' he said for about the fiftieth time, holding up a small jar of pesto.

'Yes you have. We have it on pasta all the time . . .' I pointed out.

'Not this one, we don't. This is handmade in Italy and it's got sun ripened tomatoes in it . . .'

'That's what it says on the label,' I replied. 'But I bet it's just the normal stuff only more expensive . . .'

'And this, too,' he said, putting the pesto back and picking up a bottle of chilli oil.

'But it's just olive oil with chillies in it.' I told him.

'Sounds good to me.'

I sighed. 'Mum made some last year and you never touched it.'

He looked at me and shook his head. 'Nah – if there had been this kind of oil at home I would have used it,' he told me.

'Oh shut up you stupid old man . . .'

I pushed our trolley on up the aisle, narrowly avoiding an old dear who tried to ram into my side.

'Oh, watch out!' I shouted.

The old dear stuck two fingers up at me and went on her way, mumbling something in Hindi. I steered into the next aisle, where the cans of baked beans and tuna were and walked straight into Imtiaz's mum.

'Hello Suky!' she beamed at me. Behind her I saw Imi with his dad, looking at something on the shelf.

'Hi!' I said, as my stomach dropped down to my feet and it suddenly got harder to breathe.

'Are you OK – you look ill?' Imi's mum asked.

I gulped down some air and tried to stay calm. My dad was only on the next aisle. 'I'm fine – just bored with the shopping . . .' I half-lied.

Mrs Dhondy smiled and then looked over my shoulder.

'Ah! Mrs Dhondy,' said my dad, so loud that everyone in the entire place stopped to stare. Well, OK – maybe not *everyone*. Imi and his dad heard him though.

'And how are you?' continued my dad, as Imi and his father walked up to us.

'Fine, Mr Singh,' replied Imi's mum. 'And you?'

'Can't complain,' said my dad, shaking Imi's dad's hand and having the same conversation over again.

I tried to smile at Imi but it came out all wonky and wrong.

'Hey,' he said, looking out of the corner of his eye at my dad and then back at me.

'And Imtiaz . . . looking fit and strong!' boomed my dad. Foghorn in shorts – that's what he is.

'Hi Mr Singh . . .' Imi replied, looking all shy.

'We never see you any more,' continued my dad. 'You used to come over all the time . . . grown up now though, eh? Got other things on your mind . . .'

'Er . . . yeah,' said Imi.

Mr Dhondy asked after my mum and then told me how tall I was getting.

'You'll be just like your dad, won't she, Randeep?'

My dad grinned.

'Not as ugly, though,' I said, smiling.

'Cheeky bleeder!' replied my dad.

I glanced at Imi again but he gave me a funny look, like he was embarrassed or something and then he looked away.

'Suky's got herself a boyfriend,' my dad told them, the idiot.

'Oh yes? That's lovely,' said Imi's mum. 'What's his name?'

'Jit . . .' said my dad.

Imi's parents looked at each other and then at their son. I thought they were going to say something negative but they didn't. Instead Imi's mum said that Imi had a girlfriend, too.

'Only natural at his age,' said my dad, still competing for the World's Loudest Voice trophy.

'Yes – that's my view entirely,' said Mr Dhondy. 'She's very similar to Suky from what my son tells me . . .'

I shot Imi a dirty look but he didn't look at me.

'Oh – then he has good taste too,' said my dad.

'You know – I always thought that these two might get together,' said Imi's mum. 'Tina and I used to joke about it . . .'

My dad shrugged. 'Probably too much like brother and sister,' he pointed out.

'Perhaps,' replied Mrs Dhondy, smiling at me.

After a few more words, Imi and his family moved on and I told him that I'd call him later.

'About that school project,' I lied.

'What school project?' he asked, the stupid boy.

'About the newspaper . . .?'

Imi registered about five seconds later.

'Oh yeah, that,' he said, sounding completely guilty. He was no good at this secretive lark.

'I've got a lot of questions for you,' I said, sharply. 'And I'd love to know all about this new girlfriend of yours.'

'You mean to say that he hasn't told you?' asked his mum.

'No – he must have forgotten.' I said.

'I think he's made her up,' joked Mr Dhondy.

That was when my heart tried to force it's way out of my nostrils. I was so relieved when me and dad walked away to finish our shopping.

Later on I told my mum that we'd bumped into the Dhondys.

'Oh – how nice. How was Mariam? I haven't spoken to her for ages . . .'

'She's fine,' I said.

'Did you tell her our good news?'

'Oh it's good news now then?' I asked.

'Always was, although we haven't told your gran yet . . .' she told me.

'And . . .?'

'And we don't want her to find out just yet so keep that big mouth of yours shut when she's around,' she warned.

'But she's nuts – she won't know what I'm on about,' I argued.

My mum shifted in her chair and changed the subject. 'I should really call Mariam – tell her about the baby,' she said.

'I could tell Imi if you like?'

'You mean you haven't already?' she asked, looking surprised.

I shook my head. 'Only the girls . . . it's far too embarrassing,' I said.

'Oh Suky don't be such a nerd!'

'MUM!'

She smiled and told me to make her a cup of tea. I went into the kitchen where my gran was peeling an onion.

'What's that for?' I asked her in Punjabi, the only language she could speak.

'What's it to you?' she snapped, not looking at me.

'Gran!'

She turned to me and pointed the little knife she was using threateningly.

'I know,' she told me. 'Don't think I don't know . . .

you're all after my money. Trying to kill me with poisoned food . . .'

'You're totally bonkers,' I told her, this time in English.

'See?' she shouted. 'You talk to me in that peasant language . . . I *know*!'

And with that she left the kitchen, taking her onion and the knife with her. I stood where I was for a moment and imagined her stabbing us all to death and then drinking our blood. But that was the kind of thing Grace would imagine so I shook my head, stopped being so silly and made the tea, wondering all the while whether insanity ran in our family.

Imi rang me later that evening, asking me if I wanted to go out for a while.

'OK – where shall we meet?' I asked.

'Down by the shops, round the corner from Grace's?' he suggested.

'Cool. I'll be ten minutes.'

We met outside a bookshop called Browsers and walked past the rest of the shops, down an alleyway and onto Holmfield Avenue, which led down onto Holmfield Road. There was a little brook that ran under the road and we stood by it and had a snog. Then we sat on a wall and talked about stuff. I told him about the trip to seaside that my dad had planned and that I'd asked Jit to come along.

'This pretence is gonna have to stop soon,' he told me.

'I know . . .' I replied, looking down at the brook.

'You're going to have to tell them . . .'

'Well what about you and your "girlfriend" – what's that all about?' I asked.

'They don't know it's you,' he admitted. 'But they want to meet my girlfriend and I'm having to tell almost as many lies as you.'

'I'm not lying exactly,' I protested.

Imi shrugged. 'Yeah – you're just jugglin',' he said, quietly.

'I'm sorry,' I told him, before taking his hand in mine.

'You and Jit just seem to be getting closer and closer. I feel like I'm being left behind,' he said.

'But you're my boyfriend,' I replied. 'I don't want to go out with Jit. He's a really nice lad – different when you get to know him but I don't like him in that way . . .'

I leant across and kissed him a few times, not noticing the two bikes pull up across the road. When I did look over I saw Justin Patel and his even uglier friend, Andy.

They were sneering at us and for a moment I thought

they were going to come over and bother us but they didn't. They just rode off, laughing.

'They're horrible,' I told Imi, when they had gone.

'I know. And what's up with Andy's hair?'

'I dunno,' I admitted.

'So has Jit said yes to the family day out?' he asked, changing the subject.

'Not yet,' I said. 'I'm going to chase it up at school on Monday.'

Imi smiled and gave me another kiss before replying.

'As long as you ain't chasing *him*,' he told me, smiling again.

'Never.'

I should have given more thought to Justin and his mate but at the time I didn't realise just how nasty they really were. That would change quite soon though.

SEVEN

The following Monday I was sitting in English with Grace and Hannah, waiting for our first lesson to start when Jit walked in sporting a black eye. For a minute I thought that things had gone bad at home again but when I asked him he shrugged and said

'Justin.'

'When did he do that?' asked Grace, looking really concerned.

'Yesterday,' Jit told her. 'I was walking down Evington Road, going to Dean's and he jumped me . . .'

'Have you told anyone?' I asked. It was a stupid question though.

'I ain't grassing up no one,' he told me. 'It's finished with anyway . . .'

'You can't let him bully you like that,' insisted Grace. 'It's not fair.'

Jit shrugged. 'Fair ain't got nothing to do with it,' he said.

As he spoke Mr Herbert walked in wearing a long,

black leather coat. He looked like someone in an old war film – like a Gestapo officer or something.

'Suits his personality,' whispered Hannah.

'You're telling me,' I whispered back.

'SHUT UP!' shouted Mr Herbert.

'Are they the only words you know?' I muttered.

'I beg your pardon?' asked Herbert.

I thought really quickly about something that rhymed with what I'd just said, just like Dean would do, but nothing came to mind. Instead I just sat where I was like an idiot. Herbert walked over to our table and sneered at me with his bug eyes.

'I think detention at lunchtime for you, Miss Kaur . . .'

I looked away from him and at Jit, who was smiling.

'You're a knob, you know that?' he said to Herbert, under his breath.

'I'm sorry – something to say Jit?' asked the teacher.

'Yeah,' said Jit, louder this time. 'I said . . . why can't you just be nice to people . . .?'

Mr Herbert's face began to turn a deep red that spread slowly from his neck upwards. By the time it got to his forehead. He was fuming.

'Detention for you, too!' he squealed, trying to control himself.

Jit shrugged. 'Whatever . . .'

I turned to look at Grace who was staring straight at me. I smiled but she didn't even flinch. Knowing her, she probably thought we'd done it on purpose, just to be together at lunchtime.

'Right – enough of the cabaret . . . get your books out. NOW!' said Mr Herbert.

I was in Mr Herbert's classroom straight after my second lesson, waiting for Jit, when our English teacher walked in and smiled at me, like a weasel.

'You really shouldn't let people like Jit deflect you from your studies,' he told me.

'I don't,' I replied, looking out of the window.

'You're one of the most intelligent people in the class,' he continued. 'Don't get dragged down by a waster like Jit . . .'

I span my head round and looked at him in disgust. How could he call someone he was supposed to be teaching a waster? If he already had that view of Jit – then how could he teach him properly? I wanted to ask him but knew that it would only get me into more trouble. So I said nothing and returned to looking out of the window. Jit walked in a few seconds afterwards and I smiled at him.

'All right, Suky?' he said, sitting down on the chair next to mine.

'Yeah,' I replied with a smile.

Mr Herbert told us to keep quiet and said that he was going to leave us there for a while.

'The door is open and Mr Singh is only in the next room so if you start messing about . . .' he warned.

'Yeah, yeah,' murmured Jit.

'And there'll be two more pupils joining you in about five minutes. Now sit quietly and think about why you're here today . . . how you can improve your behaviour until it fits the notion of "civilised".'

'Whatever you say, you get me?' said Jit.

Mr Herbert shook his head and walked out of the room.

'Why can't you just keep quiet when he's around?' I asked Jit.

'Because he's an idiot,' he replied.

'Yeah – he is. But all you do is get into trouble all the time. Don't you want to do well at school?'

'Yeah – I do but not if I have to pretend that people like him are OK. He hates me anyway.'

I was about to say that he didn't but stopped when I remembered what Herbert had said about Jit. Instead I changed the subject.

'My dad wants to know if you can come on our family day out,' I told him.

Jit shrugged. 'I dunno, Suky. Grace is being funny with me and Imi keeps giving me dirty looks. I reckon we should come clean . . .'

'But just this one last time,' I pleaded. 'I'm going to tell them soon anyway. Me and dad saw Imi and his family shopping at the weekend and they get on really well. I think my old man would be OK—'

'So, tell him that I'm just your blag boyfriend then.'

I sighed. 'I *will* . . . after the trip maybe . . .'

'But . . .'

'*Please*, Jit . . .'

He looked at me and then winked.

'OK . . . but this is the last time for definite,' he told me.

'Promise,' I said. 'It'll be so cool to finally stop pretending that *you're* my boyfriend and tell them about Imtiaz . . .'

Jit raised an eyebrow. 'Why? What's wrong with me?' he asked, pretending to be sad.

'Oh, don't be such a dickhead,' I told him.

He got up and, before I could stop him, grabbed me in a shoulder lock, tickling me.

'Who you callin' dickhead?' he asked, as I struggled to get away.

I managed to get my arms around his middle and drag him towards me but he had a good hold on me. I don't like being outdone by boys, so I started struggling even more and in the end I fell backwards off the chair and onto the floor, with Jit on top of me. He soon let me go after that, going red in the face and scrambling off me.

'Sorry,' he muttered.

'It's OK,' I told him. 'Not like you're strong or anything . . .'

'You can say that again,' came a sneering voice from the door.

We looked up and saw Justin and Andy standing in the doorway, smiling like vultures that have spotted a dead animal.

'We could see you was busy,' said Andy. 'We didn't want to disturb you . . .'

He smiled this nasty smile at me again and I wanted to be sick. Then I caught sight of his hair, which was black with a big white patch right in the middle.

'Who does your hair,' I heard myself saying. 'A senile gorilla with a bottle of bleach?'

Andy stepped towards us and Jit stood up quickly.

'Don't get your knickers in a twist,' said Justin, behind him. 'We're not here for you. We've got detention with that shithead Herbert . . .'

Jit didn't say anything, but Justin and Andy sat down and continued to look at us.

Justin sneered. 'That eye looks bad, Jit. Someone hit you?'

Jit pulled a chair out next to me and sat down, ignoring Justin, as Mr Herbert walked back into the room. I'd never been so pleased to see him. Justin spent the rest of the detention watching me. Even when I wasn't looking in his direction, which was most of the time, I could feel his eyes on me. It wasn't a good feeling.

The bad feeling I'd had got worse between my final two lessons. I was walking out of the loos when I saw Justin and Andy standing by a radiator. I tried to walk past but Andy stood in my way. He was almost as ugly as Justin. He had one of those wispy moustaches that some boys get and a big mole next to his nose, with a long hair growing out of it. There was a musty, sweaty smell coming from him.

'Get out of my way,' I told him.

He grinned at me, showing off disgusting yellow teeth.

He really was minging.

'I said move—'

Justin stepped towards me as Andy stayed where he was. I looked around but there was no one else in the corridor and I started to get scared. Justin smiled before he spoke.

'You're a right slag,' he told me. 'I mean *two* boyfriends – what's that all about?'

'Yeah . . . proper slapper, you get me?' added Andy. His breath smelt bad, like maybe he had a dead animal in his mouth and I wanted to throw up.

'You don't know anything about me,' I told them, defiantly.

'Yes we do. One day we see you with that Imtiaz, snogging him up in broad daylight; and the next, you're all over Jit . . .' said Justin.

'But . . .' I began.

'So, we asked around and a couple of lads in your class told us what we wanted to know, Suky . . . Although they had to be persuaded . . .' he cut in.

'Now, what would happen if your parents found out about Jit?' said Andy.

'Serious trouble, I reckon,' added Justin.

I couldn't help glaring at him, even though I didn't want him to see that I was worried.

'And seein' as how we followed you home the other day when you were feeling up Imtiaz . . . it's not like we don't know where to post an anonymous letter . . .' he threatened.

'Get lost!' I replied.

'Won't cost you much . . . twenty quid a week should do it,' said Andy. 'Your parents must be rich – yer house is big enough.'

'You think I'm going to pay you?' I said. 'You're mad.'

Justin stepped right into my face.

'Either you pay or we tell your parents about how much you lie and we'll tell Imtiaz what you were doing with Jit during detention . . .'

I glared at him. 'You stupid—' I started.

'You got until Friday to get us the money . . .' said Andy, cutting me off, before they both smiled again and walked off, leaving me in shock.

There was no way I was going to give them my money but I couldn't risk them telling my parents or Imtiaz anything. I was in trouble.

EIGHT

The next morning before registration I told Grace and Hannah most of what had happened, but not everything. I didn't mention that Justin and Andy had seen me rolling around the floor with Jit. Grace would have *loved* that. Instead I told them that they had threatened to lie to Imi about me and Jit.

'What kind of lies?' asked Grace.

'They're gonna tell Imi that they saw me and Jit snogging but that never happened . . .' I told her.

'So, they're just making it all up, are they?' she replied.

'Yes!'

'Just so that you'll give them money?' added Hannah.

'Exactly. And they actually followed me home, too, so they know where I live.'

'That's just creepy,' said Hannah. 'Can't you tell a teacher?'

'And say what? It's their word against mine – no one else was in the corridor.'

'And you really *haven't* been seeing Jit too?' asked Grace.

'Grace . . . I just told you the truth . . .'

She looked at me, raised an eyebrow and then shrugged.

'OK – I believe you,' she said. 'We're going to have to tell the lads though.'

'Why?' I asked.

'Because that way they won't believe any lies that those two ugly shits come up with,' Hannah pointed out.

'Forewarned is forearmed and all that . . .' added Grace.

'But what if they tell my parents?'

'That's another problem entirely,' replied Grace.

'So, what are we going to do about it,' I asked.

Both of my friends shrugged.

'Dean and Jit are always good for coming up with ideas . . . let's have a conference round at Grace's later . . .' suggested Hannah.

'Yeah!' agreed Grace. 'Surely we can come up with something between us? I mean – those two bullies are thicker than pig poo . . .'

'Whale poo, even,' added Hannah.

'Elephant and whale poo *together* isn't as thick as them,' said Grace.

Mrs Dooher walked in and said hello to us as I sat and thought about what we were going to do. I suppose it was my fault for lying to my parents but that still didn't excuse what Justin and Andy were doing. I wanted to go and kick them in their heads, I was so angry.

'How did it go with Matt?' asked Mrs Dooher, disrupting my thoughts.

'Huh?'

'Matt . . . the *new* boy?' she said.

I'd totally forgotten about him.

'Er . . . he was OK,' I told her. 'We showed him around and then he did his own thing, kind of . . .'

Mrs Dooher shook her head.

'You mean you ignored him from then on . . .'

'Not exactly,' I said, trying to remember the last time I had seen him, which was when he'd been talking to Robert and Wesley about those silly books that they all loved.

'I think he's hanging around with Robert and Wesley from 8CM, Miss.'

'Yeah he is,' added Grace. 'I saw him this morning. They were talking about science . . . he's going to fit right in with them.'

'Oh, good,' replied Mrs Dooher, genuinely.

'Do I get an award for integrating him so successfully into our school?' I asked her.

'You should get an award for the skinniest legs!' shouted a lad called Paresh. I turned round and gave him a filthy look.

'Oooh – I'm scared,' he said in a girly voice.

I waited until Mrs Dooher was distracted before I made my move. I got up and walked over to Paresh. He smiled at me, as if to ask what I was going to do that was so bad. I shot out my arm, grabbed his big, long nose and twisted it. 'OWWWWWWW!!!'

The rest of his mates started laughing and Mrs Dooher looked up from what she was doing.

'Are you beating up the boys, again?' she asked.

'Yes, Miss,' I replied, grinning because I knew what was coming.

'Oh good,' said Mrs Dooher. 'Saves me a job . . .'

I didn't even make it to lunchtime before Justin and Andy lived up to their threats. I was walking into my CDT class when I saw Imi. He was holding Jit by his throat and pushing him up against a wall. Dean was trying to pull them apart. I ran over and grabbed Imi's arm, shouting at him to let go.

'What's going on – stop it!' I shouted.

'I *know* you've been seeing my girl!' spat Imi, right into Jit's face.

Jit shoved Imi back and between me and Dean we managed to make him let go, only Imi didn't calm down. Instead he turned on me.

'You were *seen* – kissing Jit,' he told me angrily.

'No I *wasn't* – it's a lie . . .' I told him.

'Why would they lie?' he asked. 'They saw you . . .'

'*Who*?' asked Dean, holding Jit back with one hand.

Jit was going mad, swearing and trying to get at Imi.

'Cool it!' Dean shouted at him.

'This is all wrong,' I said, trying not to cry.

'Well what happened then?' demanded Imi.

'It was Justin and Andy – they've been threatening me. They said that if I didn't give them money they'd tell you a load of lies . . .'

Imi thought about it for a moment, just enough time for Jit to jump on him.

'*OI*!' shouted Dean, pulling Jit off.

'You knob,' Jit spat at Imi. 'You think I'm scared of you?'

I grabbed Jit by the hand and told him to stop. 'It's not his fault . . . it was Justin . . .' I repeated.

'So?' replied Jit. 'He could have asked me first. Instead

he jumped me like he's some bad bwoi . . . ain't no one grabbing me up like that!'

The rest of the pupils were beginning to come into the classroom and they looked shocked. Apart from Marco that is. He told Jit to smack Imi.

'I'm going to stick your head in a vice in a minute,' Dean warned.

Marco went red and looked at the floor.

'Just calm down,' Dean then said to Imi and Jit. 'Otherwise I'm gonna bang *both* of you out . . .'

'It isn't what you think,' I told Imi, who was beginning to calm down.

'Then what is it?' he asked me.

'A lie – that's all . . . I was telling Grace and Hannah about it and we were going to tell you all . . .'

'What the *hell* is going on?' shouted Mr Granger from the doorway.

'Nothing, sir,' I lied.

'Doesn't look like nothing to me,' he replied. 'Imtiaz – why is your tie all over the place?'

Imi looked at me and over at Jit. He turned to Mr Granger and shrugged.

'We were just messing about,' he told him.

'Yeah – practising rugby tackles,' added Dean. 'Like we seen the England team doing . . .'

'Jit?' asked Granger.

'Yeah – *that* was it,' snapped Jit, still angry.

I looked at him. 'Just leave it, Jit,' I whispered. 'It was a misunderstanding . . .'

He nodded at me but his eyes were glazed over and I knew he wasn't listening. As Grace and Hannah walked in, I sat down with Imi and tried to talk to him. But Mr Granger had started the lesson and Imi was ignoring me. Instead, I wrote a note for Grace, telling her what had happened and passed it along. She sent one back and then over the rest of the lesson we had a conversation that way. Grace told me that she'd talk to Dean and Jit, and ask them to come to her house after school. I agreed to do the same with Imi. We really had to sort out the mess that I'd created. I didn't want Imi and Jit to fight. We were all friends and I wanted it to stay that way.

NINE

We arranged it with Grace that Dean and Jit would arrive at her house before the rest of us. I went home first and walked straight into another problem. My dad was in the living room eating a banana and watching kids' telly.

'How 'bout this comin' Saturday?' he asked me, as I flopped down onto the sofa.

'It's the day after Friday,' I replied. 'You can't miss it . . . just wake up and there it'll be.'

'For the family day trip,' he added.

'Oh right – that.'

'Well? I've spoken to your mum and she's up for it. And your uncle Mandeep is coming too, bringing the family . . .'

'Whatever,' I replied, yawning at him.

'So, is the lad coming or not?' he said, talking about Jit.

'Er . . . yeah, I think so . . .' I was thinking about the meeting we were about to have and my dad may as well have been talking into a hurricane.

'Have you actually asked him, Suky?'

'Yeah . . .'

My dad sighed and stood up. He placed his banana skin on the coffee table.

'You been takin' drugs or summat?' he asked me.

'Don't be silly,' I replied.

'So, is he coming?'

I nodded. 'I'm going to see him later so I'll double check, but he did say he was going to come.'

'Oh good,' said my dad, with a sly smile. 'We can have lots of fun . . .'

I gave him a funny look.

'Don't be mean to him – otherwise I'll tell him not to bother,' I warned.

'Mean – me? Never. It's your gran he needs to be careful with . . .'

'*Your* mother,' I reminded him.

As if she had sensed that we'd mentioned her, my gran came walking into the room, muttering under her breath.

'What's that Mum?' asked my dad in Punjabi.

'Nothing you need to hear,' she told him. 'Isn't this witch supposed to be at school?' she added, talking about me.

'She's been and come back,' he told her.

'Finished already?' replied my gran. 'What kind of school is it? They should beat them with sticks . . . straighten them right out.'

'Not in this country,' I told her, speaking in English because I knew she'd react.

'Shall I paint your face white?' she asked me in Punjabi. 'Talking to me in that silly language all the time.'

Then she looked at my dad, farted twice and walked out of the room, talking to my granddad, who'd been dead since I was four years old.

'You going to put that in the bin?' I asked my dad.

'What . . . your gran?' he replied, with a grin.

'No, you fool. The banana skin . . .' I told him, laughing.

'Nah – give you something to do instead of sitting on your arse all day watching telly,' he said.

'Look who's talking . . .'

'I'm off to work now,' he replied. 'Someone's gotta pay for your expensive tastes . . .'

'Oh go and eat another banana,' I told him.

He walked out of the room, doing a bad impression of an ape. The weirdo.

* * *

Grace's dad opened the door to me, Imi and Hannah about an hour later. He was wearing an apron and yellow rubber gloves.

'Hi, Mr Parkhurst,' said Hannah.

'Hello – please excuse the outfit. I was cleaning the bath . . .'

'No problem,' I told him.

'They're downstairs playing pool,' he told us before wandering back upstairs.

Grace's parents had turned their cellar into a proper room when we were all kids and it was massive. It ran almost the entire length of their house and the ceiling was quite high. There were sofas down there, along with a telly and hi-fi; and a pool table that the lads always hogged whenever we visited, which was all the time. Especially Jit, who seemed to spend more time at Grace's house than his own.

As we made our way downstairs, I hoped that Jit wouldn't throw a fit when he saw Imi. Grace hadn't told him we were coming and I didn't want it to be an unpleasant surprise. It wasn't. Jit nodded at Imi when he saw him and Imi said hello. It was all cold and macho but then what did I expect from boys. It's not like they were going to hug each other or something.

'You made it then?' said Grace, as I joined her on a sofa.

'Yeah,' I replied.

Dean was bent across the table, about to take a shot when Hannah tried to put him off.

'Like two pigs fighting in a sack,' she said to us.

'What is?' I asked.

'Dean's ass . . . it's huge!' she replied.

Dean missed his shot by a mile and turned to her. 'See? You just put me off, Hannah.'

'Well your *ass* was putting me off,' she told him.

Dean grinned. 'No it wasn't. You love it . . . I seen the way you look at it . . . well you can look, darlin' because yuh nah get none ah me . . .'

Hannah pretended that she was puking.

'You can keep it,' she said, when she'd stopped pretending.

'Yeah,' added Grace. 'He can keep it from falling *out* with a harness and a big tarpaulin.'

'*Huge* tarpaulin,' said Hannah.

'Giant . . . big enough to hold a *tank* . . .'

Dean just grinned again. 'If I had known it was pick on Dean day – I would have stayed at home,' he said.

I smiled and looked over at Jit and Imi. They were standing at opposite ends of the table, not talking and not looking at each other either. I caught Jit's eye and nodded my head towards Imi, hoping that he'd make the first move. Some chance. Jit just shrugged and looked away. In the end, as Dean, Grace and Hannah continued to tease each other, I decided to get things going.

'We need to talk,' I said, in my loudest voice.

'Someone let a ferry in here?' asked Dean. 'I heard a foghorn . . .'

'Listen you chicken-legged, wannabe-but-can't-rhyme rapper – this is serious,' I replied.

'*Oooh* – let's all sit down because Suky says so,' added Hannah.

'Oh come on – it's not funny,' I told them seriously.

Everyone looked at me and shut up. Hannah and Dean went and sat on the other sofa and Jit and Imi stayed where they were.

'So what's goin' on?' asked Dean.

'What do you mean – what's going on?' asked Grace. 'Just the little matter of two of us trying to beat each other to a pulp at school – that's all.'

'Weren't *my* fault,' said Jit.

'Weren't mine either,' added Imi.

I sighed. 'It wasn't either of you. It was all down to Justin Patel and his smelly mate . . .'

'He *does* smell, doesn't he?' said Grace. 'And what's the deal with that hair?'

Dean smirked. 'I know how that happened,' he told us. 'This girl I know, in Year Ten – she told me . . .'

'What – one of your pretend women?' asked Hannah.

'No pretence at all, my dear,' replied Dean, in a posh accent.

'So how did it happen?' asked Jit.

Dean sat up on the sofa and cleared his throat like he was about to tell us something really important.

'That Andy was watchin' some telly show and decided that he wanted to have bleached hair, just like one of the characters. Thought it'd help him pull girls and that. He told Justin and Justin said that he'd do it for him. Told him it was easy and he'd done it before. So Andy takes his skinny, no-ass body round to Justin's and they start trying to bleach his hair . . .'

'They tried to use a home bleaching kit?' I asked.

Dean shook his head. 'Nah – that would have been too normal,' he told us.

'So, what *did* they use?' asked Imi, smiling at me.

'Domestos,' replied Dean, with a grin.

'*NO*!' shouted Hannah.

'*Yeah* – Justin poured a load of Domestos over Andy's head and when it started to burn his scalp he ran out of the house screaming. They had to take him to hospital . . .'

'But couldn't he just shave his head and let it grow back as his natural colour?' asked Grace.

Dean shook his head.

'Nah – the girl I know told me that he's damaged summat permanently and it won't go back to normal . . .'

'That's just stupid,' said Hannah.

'Very stupid,' I added. 'But none of this helps us sort out the mess we're in.'

'You mean the mess *you're* in?' asked Grace.

'Whatever,' I replied. 'Can we try and sort it out please?'

Dean slumped back again.

'OK,' he said, 'although I was about to tell you another story I know . . .'

'About Justin and Andy?' asked Grace, excitedly.

'Nah – bout this next idiot . . .'

'*Dean*!' I snapped.

'OK, OK. No need to get your size eighteen panties in a twist . . .' he replied.

TEN

'So what we going to do then?' I asked.

'Dunno,' replied Grace.

'What did they say to you exactly?' asked Dean.

'They said that they'd tell Imtiaz that I was seeing Jit too,' I began.

'Well, they already done that,' said Jit. 'And macho-man over there reacted too.'

Imi tensed up but then calmed straight down.

'I know he was wrong to have a go at you,' said Grace, 'but he didn't know they were lying . . .'

Jit had probably been expecting Grace to back him up. I think it made him pay attention a bit more.

'And if someone had told me that my boyfriend was seen snogging some other girl, I would have reacted the same way,' she added.

'Can't see you grabbing someone by the throat and holding them against a wall,' Dean pointed out.

'Oh, you know what I mean,' replied Grace, seriously.

'So, we need to square that first,' said Hannah. She

looked at Jit and Imi in turn.

'Don't look at me,' said Imi. 'He jumped me after I'd stopped and anyway – I'm not the one going on and on about it.'

'Oh don't be such a child,' I told him. 'Both of you are to blame for the way you reacted but neither of you started it. That was Justin and Andy . . .'

'But I never done anything wrong,' Jit pointed out. 'Why should I get grief . . . he grabbed my throat for no reason . . .'

'We *have* been spending a lot of time together,' I told him. 'And we were messing about when they saw us . . .'

It was a gamble, being honest about what Justin and Andy had seen but I decided that I didn't have anything to hide. After all, as I'd said, me and Jit had been messing about. Jit went a bit red as Imi gave me a quizzing look.

'What do you mean *messing* about?' he asked.

'Jit was tickling me,' I admitted. 'It was just a bit of fun, that's all . . .'

'*Tickling* you? And you think that's OK?' he snapped.

'Oh – don't be a such a baby,' said Grace. 'You pinched my bottom last week.'

This time Imi went red.

'Oh *yeah*?' I said.

'I only did it because you *asked* me too,' Imi told

Grace. 'You were going on about having buns of steel . . .'

'Yeah – but the point is it was just a laugh,' Grace said. 'We didn't end up snogging or anything. It didn't *mean* anything . . .'

'I know,' replied Imi.

'So what's the big deal with Jit tickling me?' I asked Imi. 'We're all friends, aren't we?'

Imi looked at Jit and then back at me. 'I suppose so,' he said, sheepishly.

'*Jit*?' asked Dean, his first serious input into our conversation.

'*What*?' replied Jit.

'We are all mates, *ain't* we?' Dean asked.

'Yeah – I never said we weren't. I just don't like being grabbed up like that.'

'Well in that case – I'm sorry,' said Imi.

Hannah grinned. 'God, that took ages,' she said.

'I'm sorry too,' said Jit. 'For jumping on you and that . . .'

'*Ahh*! Now are you going to kiss and make up?' asked Grace.

'I said we were mates,' replied Jit, in disgust. 'But I ain't kissin' his ugly raas . . .'

'No *way*,' said Imi.

'You should at least shake hands,' suggested

'Whatever,' said Imi, walking over to Jit and sh
his hand.

'Would have kicked yer ass though,' Jit told him, grinning.

'With *those* skinny arms – doubt it . . .' replied Imi.

And that was it. They were back to being friends and stopped sulking. All that left was to talk about what else Justin had said. Hannah picked up on it.

'They threatened something else too, didn't they?' she asked me.

'*What*?' asked Dean.

I nodded. 'Yeah – they said that they'd tell my parents about Imi and Jit. They said they'd tell Imi's parents too.'

'*Shit*!' said Imi, just as Grace's dad came down the stairs carrying a tray.

'Anyone for drinks?' he asked. He was wearing a really cool T-shirt that said 'God Is Too Big For Just One Religion'. Above the words were six small circles, each one carrying the symbol of a different world religion.

'Er . . . yeah Dad,' replied Grace. 'Thanks. Just put them down on the table . . .'

'Oh, right,' replied Mr Parkhurst, looking upset. 'I can see I'm not wanted . . .'

'Dad,' groaned Grace. 'We're having a private conversation.'

Mr Parkhurst smiled. 'A private conversation – all *six* of you?' he asked.

'Yes,' Grace told him. 'Now *shoo*!'

Mr Parkhurst shrugged and went back upstairs. 'Your dad's T-shirt is wicked,' said Dean, beating me to the punch. 'Where'd he get it?'

'Dunno,' said Grace. 'And that's beside the point. We were talking about Justin and Andy . . .'

'So what do they want?' asked Imi, looking worried.

'Twenty quid – every week . . .'

'*Nah*! That's just daylight robbery, you get me,' said Jit. 'Were they wearing masks and that?'

'It's not that much money – between us,' said Grace.

I shook my head. 'I'm not giving them anything,' I said.

'But what if they carry out their threat?' asked Imi.

'I'm going to tell my parents the truth before that . . .' I told them.

'*When*?' asked Jit.

'After the weekend . . .'

Grace gave me a funny look. 'So what are you going to do about the money this week?' she asked.

'Nothing,' I replied. 'My parents are out all night on

Friday and on Saturday we're all going on a day trip to the seaside . . .'

'*This* Saturday?' asked Jit.

'Yeah – sorry I was going to tell you . . .'

Imi and Grace both pulled a face each.

'Is Jit going on this one *too*?' asked Imi.

'Yeah – this is the last one though,' I said. 'I promise. I'll tell them on Sunday. Justin and Andy won't get the chance to get to them before me.'

'Are you sure?' asked Jit, looking concerned.

'Absolutely . . .' I told him.

Dean stood up and went over to the pool table, picking up the cue ball and turning it in his hand as he spoke.

'We're gonna have to get clever with Justin and Andy,' he said.

'How do you mean?' asked Hannah.

'Well they've got it in for Suky, me, Jit *and* Imi. We're gonna have to stop them somehow . . .'

'You could always tell Gussie,' suggested Jit, talking about Dean's older brother.

Dean shook his head.

'Nah – Gussie will go and get all medieval on 'em . . . and get into trouble. It's got to be something clever and slick . . . like in the movies,' he replied.

'And who's going to come up with that plan then?' asked Imi.

'Me,' said Dean. 'Just let me think about it . . .'

I looked at him and sighed. 'Just don't go getting into trouble. Like I told you – I'll tell my parents at the weekend,' I said.

Dean shook his head again. 'This is going to take longer than a few days, if I'm honest. It's gonna have to be more of a long-term plan . . .'

I wondered what he was on about but left it. An hour later Imi walked me part of the way home and when I went to bed that night I thought about how I was going to tell my parents about my deception. Which words I was going to use and how I was going to use them. I rehearsed my opening line in my head, over and over until I fell asleep.

ELEVEN

I was with Hannah the next morning, walking down to Registration, when Justin approached me.

'Got my money?' he asked, nastily.

'No,' I replied, as Hannah started to look worried.

'Well you've got until tomorrow,' he told me.

'But you said Friday,' I reminded him, trying not to sound like I was bothered, even though I was.

He smirked at me and I wanted to punch him. But I don't do that. I may beat the boys at sports all the time but I'm not violent.

'I changed my mind,' he told me, all self-importantly, as if he was God or something. The ugly, rat-faced zero.

'Well I haven't got it and I can't get it until Friday so you're gonna have to wait . . .' I replied, trying this time to sound defiant.

'Thursday – or the parents get a nice, anonymous letter or maybe even a knock at the door . . .'

This time I smirked.

'You turn up at my door and my dad will kick your ass,' I warned.

He thought about it for a moment and I could tell he was concerned. Then he put his rat-face back on and smiled.

'Well then it'll be a letter . . .'

'Why don't you just get lost?' asked Hannah.

'Or go and play with a bottle of Domestos?' I added, feeling more confident. It didn't last long.

Justin scowled and grabbed my bag from me. As I tried to get it off him, he opened it and emptied my stuff all over the floor of the corridor. The other pupils stopped and stared at us. I looked down and saw all my things on the floor. Some little shit started laughing behind me.

'*Ehh*! Who comes to school with deodorant?' he squealed.

'From the way you smell – not you, obviously,' snapped Hannah.

The year seven lad looked at her in shock as his friends started laughing at him. I didn't join in. Justin opened my bag wider and then did something really nasty. He cleared his throat and spat into it. Then he threw it back at me and I caught it.

'Tomorrow, or I'll have to get really angry,' he warned, as he walked away.

I dropped my bag and then fell to my knees to collect my things. I had tears in my eyes and when Hannah knelt to help me, I turned my face away.

'He's so gonna get it,' she told me. 'I don't care when and I don't care how – but it's gonna happen . . .'

I carried on picking up my stuff.

'Are you OK?' she asked.

'No!' I snapped. 'He spat in my bag!'

And then I started crying which made me even angrier than I was. Hannah picked up the last of my things and helped me into the girl's loo. I put all my stuff on the sink surround and wiped my eyes.

'Want me to clean your bag for you?' asked Hannah.

'No . . . but thanks for offering.'

'I don't mind, honestly,' she added.

I shook my head.

'Just leave it. I don't want it any more – I'll get another,' I told her.

'Well, you're going to need something to carry your things in for the rest of today,' she pointed out.

'Oh . . .' I said. I hadn't even thought about that.

Hannah grinned at me via the mirror that I was staring into. She opened her bag and got a plastic bag out, from the supermarket where her mum works. She handed it to me.

'I know it's not exactly Louis Vuitton,' she said, 'but it'll do the job.'

I turned to her and gave her a big hug.

'Whoa sister . . . a thank you will suffice,' she joked, even though she hugged me back.

'I hate him,' I told her, after I'd let her go.

'You and everyone else in this school . . .'

I swore a few times.

'Suky! Young ladies don't say things like that,' teased Hannah.

'Stuff that,' I replied. 'Let's get to Registration and please don't tell anyone what happened. Please . . .'

'Not even Grace and the lads?' she asked.

'Especially not them. Promise me,' I demanded.

'I promise,' she told me.

I began to put my stuff into the bag and wondered about getting some of my big, nasty cousins to beat up Justin for me. But having them kick seven shades of you-know-what out of him wouldn't make me feel better. I'd only be happy if I handled it myself. Or with a little help from my friends. I decided to ask Dean what he had come up with. One way or another, Justin Patel and Andy Stevenson were going to get theirs. Even if it took the rest of the school year for it to happen.

* * *

I know it sounds mean but I only cheered up at lunchtime, when Robert and Wesley walked into the room where we prepare the school newspaper. I'm not a mean person but somehow talking to Robert and Wesley made me laugh. They were sweet in their own way, but they were also *so* easy to tease. Only Grace and me were in the classroom when the two of them arrived. They said that Mr Black wanted us to interview them immediately for the paper. Grace sighed and shook her head.

'Does he realise how much I've got to do?' she joked. 'I've got deadlines pouring out of my nose like watery snot and a print run to deal with and celebrities to slander . . .'

'It'll only take a little while,' said Robert.

'*Only a little while*?' repeated Grace. 'I don't *have* a little while, as you so naively put it. This is the high-pressure world of print media, my lad. No room for sentiment or farting around . . .'

'But . . .'

I decided that I'd join in too. 'I suppose *I'll* have to do it,' I told them. 'I've got the prime minister on the other line but I'll just have to put him on hold . . .'

'You're doing an article on the *prime* minister?' asked Wesley, looking excited.

'What do *you* think, you silly boy?' asked Grace.

'We're teasing you,' I told them, as Wesley went bright red, which was only a slight change for him because his face was always red. He pushed his glasses up on the bridge of his nose.

'Oh – I see,' said Robert, smiling. 'Humour . . . something which pervades the series of novels we adore . . .'

Grace tried to stop herself laughing but only managed it by kicking her right shin with her left foot.

'*OWWW*!'

'Is something the matter, Grace?' asked Robert, looking very concerned.

'Oh – it's nothing,' Grace told him. 'Just a little involuntary twitch. Runs in the family, I'm afraid . . .'

'My family has a history of mild insanity,' offered Wesley.

'*Really*?' I asked, stepping on my own toe to stop the laughter.

'Yes – it's very strange. Seems to appear at random . . .' he continued.

'That's all well and good, Mr Magoogan,' said Robert, trying to show authority, 'but we are here to be interviewed about chess . . .'

'*Exactly*,' agreed Grace. 'How lovely that we think along the same lines, Robert.'

I knew that she was still teasing but Robert has a massive crush on Grace and he smiled so broadly that I thought he might swallow his own ears.

'Erm . . . I . . . I . . . yes . . . er . . .' he stammered, which was like his default setting whenever Grace was nice to him.

Grace stood up and went over to him, leaning in to his left ear.

'So, what can I help you with?' she whispered.

Robert pulled back slightly and almost giggled.

'Erm . . . er . . . haha . . .' he mumbled.

'Perhaps we could start with a little chat about your interests?' I suggested.

'What a wonderful idea,' agreed Grace, still close enough to Robert that he could feel her breath against his skin. He went the same colour as Wesley; I could have sworn that I saw steam coming from his ears, too. Well, OK – maybe I didn't.

'I was thinking about that series you mentioned – *The Dark World of Lazywitch*?' I said.

Robert cleared his throat. 'I think you'll find that it's called *The Dark Lord Of Hazlewitch*,' he corrected.

'Yeah – that,' I continued. It wasn't that I didn't know what the series was called – you couldn't get away from the silly books – I just wanted Robert and Wesley to get excited about them and, true to form, they did.

'We're just re-reading the first seven books,' Wesley informed us. 'Ready for the sequels to appear on Christmas Eve . . .'

'You mentioned that a few days ago,' I said. 'What's that all about?'

'Well,' replied Robert, 'there are two sequels because Princess Wondlebarn, the heroine has had to travel back in time to before her own birth to save the people of Hazlewitch from Gerafaggan. He's the Dark Lord . . .'

'Why does the Princess have to travel back in time. Isn't there a knight in shining armour to rescue her from the drudgery of her existence and whisk her away to somewhere nice with shops?' asked Grace.

Wesley smiled. Then he unleashed a wave of information at us.

'There are rumours that she'll meet her prince in the past but they've not been verified by the author. What's happened is this – Tar, the giant rat and former friend of the Royal House Of Hazlewitch has been turned to the Dark Way by the evil Lord Gerafaggan. He has stolen the Ancient Flute Of Kings and given it to the Dark Lord. Now the Dark Lord—'

'Is Tar actually *rat* spelt backwards?' asked Grace.

'Yes – but do let me finish,' replied Wesley, the closest I'd ever seen him to being annoyed.

Obviously Hazlewitch fans were not to be trifled with, not where their precious series was concerned. Grace said '*ooh*' and continued listening.

'The Dark Lord is aware of the power vested in the Princess from the Stones of Ganjamash and he has spirited the Ancient Flute away to the distant past to keep her from it. If the Princess can get the flute then she can find all the Ganjamash Stones, bring them together and end the tyranny of the Dark Lord. But she has to find the flute first and that's where Pitchy-Patchy comes in . . .'

'Who?' I asked.

'Pitchy-Patchy. He's a magical being from the Time Beyond Time When All Things Were Equal. Equilibrium Time, it's called. Anyway, he has a magic rod, which he hides under his skirts . . .'

'Wesley – are you being *rude*?' asked Grace.

'No – why ever would you ask me that?' he replied, looking embarrassed.

'Well a magic *rod* – *under* his skirts – it all sounds a bit rude to me,' Grace told him.

'*Very* rude,' I said.

'*Ruder* than rude,' added Grace.

'Like the rudest thing you've ever heard but ten times worse . . .' I continued.

'*So* rude that if the biggest piece of rude in the *whole* world came and farted in your face, it couldn't be ruder . . .' finished Grace.

'Oh do let him finish,' said Robert.

Wesley cleared his throat, pushed his glasses back up the bridge of his nose and finished his outline of the Hazlewitch series so far.

'So, Pitchy-Patchy has been sent by the God of Ganjamash to help the Princess in her quest and he's going to use his magic rod to take her back into the past. That's where the story has got to thus far . . .'

I looked at him and wondered how it took seven books to tell the story he had just outlined. I asked him but Robert decided it was his turn to speak.

'Oh there *are* other strands to the tale but that's the *main* one. In fact there is a wonderful secondary plot featuring the Bong Monkey and his friend, Tinfoil but that's something else entirely . . .

'Oh *damn*!' said Grace. 'Would you look at the time. I must be going . . .'

'Where are *you* going?' I asked her.

'To eat something . . . I said I'd meet Hannah in the dining hall . . .'

I groaned. 'But why didn't you eat when I did . . .?' I asked.

'Wasn't hungry,' she replied, grinning slyly. 'Thank God!'

'Great!' I said, as she grabbed her stuff and walked out of the classroom.

Robert and Wesley turned to me with mad grins on their faces, like evil scientists who had just found a new specimen to play with.

'Right,' I told them loudly. 'Let's get on with this interview, then . . .'

'Yes,' replied Robert. 'But perhaps first we could tell you the story of Bong Monkey, Tinfoil and their search for the Land of The Munchie-Men . . .'

'Oh God!' I groaned, as Wesley pushed his glasses back up his face for the third time.

TWELVE

Things went back to being less funny by the time I finished school for the day. The first sign was Jit, who ran past me as I was making my out of school with Imi. Justin, with Dean following close behind, was chasing him.

'Oh what now?' I asked.

'Dunno,' said Imi, but we'd better go and see.

Here we go again. I thought as I followed Imi.

We found Jit sitting on the tennis court steps, bleeding from a cut lip and being calmed down by Dean. Again.

'Leave it, bro . . . they'll just batter you again,' Dean was saying as we joined them.

'I don't *care*!' shouted Jit. 'I'm gonna kill that Justin . . .'

Dean shoved Jit back down onto the step he was sitting on and held him there.

'What happened?' I asked.

'Justin beat him up,' Dean told me. 'Something about making him regret coming to school every day . . .'

'He wants revenge for his cousin . . .' Jit added.

'What *revenge*?' I asked. 'You didn't do anything to Jason . . .'

Dean looked away.

'Dean's brother battered him over them dodgy phones,' Jit told me, talking about an incident from a few weeks earlier.

'But didn't Jason get kicked out for beating up someone else?' asked Imi.

'Yeah, he did, but he also told Justin about me and Dean,' replied Jit.

Imi nodded.

'And now he's after both of us,' said Dean. 'Although the ugly tosser's only picking on Jit . . .'

'Have you come up with anything to stop him?' I asked.

'Not yet,' he replied. 'But give me time.'

'Jit doesn't look like he's got any time,' I pointed out.

Jit stood up and wiped the blood from his mouth onto his sleeve. 'Don't worry about me,' he said, acting all hard. 'I've been hit harder than that before . . .'

'That's *not* the point,' I told him. 'You shouldn't *have* to get beaten up all the time.'

Dean looked at me. 'Who's gonna stop it?' he asked.

'Just tell your brother,' suggested Imi.

'I can't,' said Dean. 'He'll get into trouble . . .'

'So what are we gonna do?' I asked.

'Leave it with me, like I said,' replied Dean.

I was about to say something else when Grace and Hannah ran over to us. I thought that they were concerned about Jit but I was wrong. They'd opened their big mouths once too often.

'He overheard us,' said Grace, trying to get her breath back.

'*Who*?' asked Dean.

'The Skunk . . .' panted Hannah.

'*Andy*?' said Imi.

They both nodded. Hannah wouldn't look me in the eye.

'What do you *mean* he overheard?' I asked. '*What* did he hear . . .?'

Grace looked at her feet, waiting for Hannah to speak. Hannah said nothing.

'*Well?*'

'Oh all right then!' replied Grace. 'But it wasn't our fault, OK. We didn't know he was there . . .'

'Will you just tell us what happened?' I asked, getting wound up.

'We were standing by the entrance to the art department, talking about what you said,' began Grace.

'About telling your parents before Justin and Andy could get to them.'

'Oh *no*!'

'And Andy just appeared from nowhere . . .' added Hannah.

'You *told* them?' I said, getting angry.

'*No*!' snapped Grace. 'We were just talking. How were we supposed to know that he was listening to us?'

I shook my head.

'You know what it's like in this school. Even the walls gossip . . .'

'We're sorry,' said Hannah.

'Yeah – we didn't mean it,' added Grace, looking tearful.

'That's a major help – a *huge*, great help . . .' I snapped, before feeling bad about it.

'*What* did he hear?' asked Dean.

'We were talking about how brave Suky was being for refusing to give them her money and how she was going to tell her parents about Imi and Jit; and I was saying that it was about time and . . .' said Grace.

'And he heard all of it?' I asked.

'I think so,' admitted Grace. 'I'm so sorry.'

I told her that it wasn't their fault. They didn't know

that Skunk Boy was hiding nearby. But it did give me a problem. A big one. Jit pointed it out.

'If they know that you ain't gonna pay them tomorrow, then what have they got to lose?' he asked me.

'I was just thinking the same thing,' agreed Imi.

'They ain't got no reason not to tell your parents now, have they?' Jit added.

'I know,' I replied.

'And while we been standin' around here talking about it,' said Dean, 'I bet they's already on a bus headin' for your parents' house . . .'

'Oh shit!' I said.

'No need for that kind of language, Miss Kaur,' I heard a familiar voice say behind us. It was Mr Herbert.

'No need for that *face* either,' mumbled Dean.

'I *beg* your pardon?' asked Herbert.

'Nuttin',' replied Dean. 'I wasn't talkin' to you. School's finished so you ain't got no hold over what I say anyhow . . .'

'Yeah, if I was you, I'd run along,' added Jit, grinning.

'This *is* still school property!' Herbert shouted.

'See ya!' Dean said casually.

We walked out of school and went to get the bus that went near my house. Jit, Dean and Hannah, who lived on a completely different bus route waited with me, Imi and Grace.

'Are you coming too?' asked Grace.

'*Yeah*!' said Hannah. 'We don't wanna miss out on all the fun.'

I glared at her.

'Sorry, Suky,' she replied, looking slightly ashamed. There was nothing funny about my problem. Nothing at all.

My parents were both in when I got back, with the gang in tow.

'Blimey,' said my dad, when he saw us all. 'We havin' a party?'

'We just wanted to talk about a project we're all doing together,' I lied.

'All of you?' he asked.

'Yes, Mr Singh,' said Grace.

'And how are your parents, Grace?' asked my dad.

'Cool,' she replied.

I looked at my mum who half-smiled. She looked tired.

'Has anyone called for me?' I asked her.

'Er . . . not that I know of,' she replied. 'Not since I've been at home anyway . . .'

'Yeah – since then,' I asked.

'No – why were you *expecting* someone?'

'No . . . well just these two lads from school . . .'

My dad shook his head.

'More project members?' he asked.

'Er . . . yeah . . .'

'I've been back since two,' he told me. 'No one's called round at all.'

I looked at Hannah and Grace in turn and they both looked away.

'Anything in the post?' I asked my mum.

'Usual stuff. Are you expecting something?'

I nodded. 'From a pen pal,' I lied.

'What pen pal,' she asked, getting up from the kitchen table to put her coffee mug on the side.

'Just this girl I speak to on the Net,' I said, wondering how I found it so easy to lie.

'Oh – right. First *I've* heard of it . . .'

'It's a teenager thing,' said my dad. 'Secrets . . .'

He winked at me and for a second I thought that he knew but he didn't. How could he have known when Justin and Andy hadn't been round?

My mum smiled at my friends.

'I suppose you lot'll be going upstairs to Suky's room?' she asked.

'Yeah,' said Hannah. 'Lots of work to do . . .'

'Well you'll be wanting drinks, then,' replied my mum.

She looked at Jit. 'Can you help me with the drinks, Imtiaz?' she asked, yawning.

Jit shot me a quick look and then corrected her.

'You mean Jit?' he said.

'Oh my God!' replied my mum. 'I'm doing far too many hours at work. I'm sorry, Jit . . .'

'No worries,' replied Jit.

'So,' she said, smiling at Imi and Jit. 'Perhaps you can *both* help?'

'Of course . . . Mrs . . . er . . .' began Imi.

'Tina, please, Imtiaz. I'm not used to all that formal nonsense. By the way I spoke to your mum last night . . .'

'Oh – she didn't say,' said Imi.

'Well we're having another baby,' she said, without any thought to my feelings at all. Talk about embarrassment. It was one thing to get yourself pregnant when you're old. It was another thing entirely to heap shame upon your teenage daughter too.

'And I wanted to talk to her about it,' added my mum. 'Women's stuff, you know . . .'

'*MUM*!' I shouted.

'Oh grow up, Suky . . . people have babies all the time.'

'We're *going* up to my room now,' I told her, relieved that she didn't know anything about what was going on with me, Imi and Jit.

'Would you like some sandwiches?' she asked us.

Dean looked at me, then at Jit and finally he nodded.

'Yeah! I'm starvin' . . .' he told my mum.

'Ham and cheese all right for everyone?' she asked.

'Er . . . not for me,' said Imi.

My mum smiled at him.

'I know that. I used to make your packed lunches when you were little – *remember*? Your mum and I used to take turns . . .'

'I'm a vegetarian,' added Grace. 'Hannah is too . . .'

Hannah pinched Grace on the arm.

'I'll have the ham,' she told my mum.

'But I thought you were a veggie?' moaned Grace.

Hannah grinned, as we walked up to my room.

'I *was*,' she replied. 'And then my mum cooked a big, fat, steak one day and I couldn't resist . . .'

'You stinky, smelly, *dirty* girl . . .' said Grace.

THIRTEEN

I was dreading school the next morning and prayed that I didn't bump into Justin or Andy. As I got off the bus I looked around to make sure that they weren't waiting for me and then I hurried into Registration. The corridors were busy with pupils wandering about and I kept an eye out for Andy's strange hair but I didn't see him or Justin. By the time I sat down in my form room, I was out of breath.

'What's up with *you*?' asked Puspha, one of the girls in my class.

'Nothing . . .' I replied.

'You're all out of breath,' added another girl called Heather.

'No, I'm not,' I lied, wondering where my friends were.

Heather gave me a funny look and then started asking me about the school paper. Whilst I was talking to her, Grace and Hannah walked in, with Imi right behind them.

'You OK?' asked Hannah.

'Yeah – why *shouldn't* I be?'

'We thought you might have bumped into Justin and Andy,' said Imi.

'I haven't seen them at all,' I replied. 'It's probably too early for them anyway . . .'

Grace sat down next to me and put her bag on the table in front of us.

'I hope they don't go after Jit again,' she said.

'Well, if he told the teachers what they're up to, they might stop,' I pointed out.

'So are you going to the seaside on Saturday?' she asked.

'Yeah – we're leaving really early in the morning . . .'

Hannah grinned.

'But it's October,' she said. 'It'll be freezing . . .'

I shrugged, 'That's my dad for you,' I told her. 'Weirdo . . .'

'He'll probably take you to the North Pole next summer,' teased Grace.

'Knowing him, you're probably right,' I said.

Mrs Dooher walked in with a hamster cage, covered in dark blue cloth and put it down on her desk.

'What's *that*, Miss?' asked Heather.

'It's a cage,' replied Mrs Dooher dryly. 'What does it look like?'

'Yeah, but what's in it?' said Dilip.

'A rat,' Mrs Dooher told him.

'*EHHHHHHHH*!' came a loud shout from half the classroom.

'Oh, do shut up!' Mrs Dooher half-shouted. 'It's not a wild rat . . . it's a pet.'

'*Nah*! What kind of weirdo keeps a rat as a pet?' asked Marco.

'My daughters . . .' admitted Mrs Dooher.

'Man that's just sick . . .' said Milorad.

'No it isn't,' replied Grace. 'What's the *difference* between a rat and a hamster? Or a guinea pig . . .?'

'Plenty,' said Marco.

'No there *isn't*,' protested Grace. 'And besides they're all pointless. All they do is stuff their faces, poo and run around on wheels all day . . .'

'Do they eat their poo too, like rabbits?' asked Hannah.

'I'm not sure,' replied Mrs Dooher. 'I'll have to ask my daughters.'

Marco stood up and walked over to the cage. He lifted the cloth and a little snout poked out from between the bars, shocking him.

'*AHH*!' he screamed.

'You big baby!' laughed Hannah.

…o! I wasn't scared . . .' he lied.

'Yes you were!' said Dilip. 'You're just *gay*, you are . . .'

'*DILIP*!'

The whole class stopped what they were doing and looked at Mrs Dooher in awe. She had never really raised her voice before and we were all shocked. Especially Dilip. You could have driven a bus into his gob.

'We don't use racist, sexist or homophobic language in this school – do you understand?'

'But I didn't Miss,' whined Dilip. 'I only called him gay . . .'

'That *is* homophobic, you knob,' I heard Dean say from the doorway. Jit was standing next to him. I smiled at them both.

'*No*! I'm not homo . . .!' protested Dilip.

'Dilip,' said Mrs Dooher in her usual voice. 'You were saying Marco was gay and implying that that is somehow wrong. I won't allow that. You're entitled to your opinion but when it's as nasty as that, kindly keep it to yourself. Understand?'

Dilip sighed.

'Yes, Miss. But I didn't mean it . . . I'm not homoph . . . ph . . . that thing.'

'I'm glad to hear it,' said Mrs Dooher.

'So, why *have* you brought your daughters' pet to school?' asked Hannah.

'Well – originally there were two,' she told us all. 'Mop and Bucket. But Mop died and my daughters couldn't bear to keep just Bucket on his own . . .'

'How did he die?' asked Milorad.

Mrs Dooher pulled a strange face, like she was trying not to grin. It didn't work.

'My eldest daughter, Nancy . . .' she began.

'Is she *fit*, Miss?' asked Dilip.

'Who?'

'Your daughter . . .?' he explained.

'Oh, shut up, Dilip,' replied Mrs Dooher. 'Anyway, Nancy let them out of the cage and Mop ran out of the room. He went and hid in the cellar and the other day my husband went down to get a bottle of wine . . .'

'And found him *dead*?' asked Marco, excitedly.

'Er . . . no. Not exactly,' she said. 'Fran – that's my husband – he pulled out a bottle of wine and it slipped from his hands and just at that moment poor Mop poked his head out from under the wine rack . . .'

She tried really hard not to laugh but it was no use. She cracked up and had trouble finishing the story.

'. . . He . . . he . . . said that the bottle b . . . b . . . bounced off the poor little thing's head! Squashed it flat!'

Mrs Dooher let out a shriek of laughter and we all followed. When she'd calmed herself down, she told us the rest.

'So anyway, Katie – that's my youngest – and Nancy, agreed to let your class take care of Bucket and here he is.'

She lifted the cloth off the cage. Heather screamed. Dilip giggled and Marco fainted. I looked at Jit whilst all this was happening and asked him about Saturday.

'I'm sorted,' he told me. 'My mum's going to drop me off round the corner from yours early . . .'

'Why not at the door?' I asked.

'*DOH*! What if your dad sees her? Starts asking her questions?'

'Oh yeah . . .' I said, as Mrs Dooher tried to revive Marco. The big wuss.

I didn't see Justin or Andy at all that day and when I was on my way home I pointed it out to Grace and Imi.

'Don't you think it's a bit weird?' I said.

'Maybe they were just bunking off?' suggested Grace.

'On the day that they said they wanted me to give them money? I doubt it,' I replied.

'Well, they did overhear Grace and Hannah saying that you wouldn't do that,' said Imi.

'No – that doesn't make sense either . . .' I replied.

Then I had a terrible thought.

'What if they went round to my house today?'

'Oh,' said Imi.

'Ploppy pants . . .!' added Grace.

'What if my parents are waiting for me right now – ready to batter me for lying to them? I think I'm going to be sick . . .' I said.

'You don't even know that's what's happened,' replied Grace, trying to reassure me.

'I don't know that it hasn't either,' I pointed out.

When I got in my parents *were* waiting for me but they didn't let rip when I walked into the kitchen. Instead they asked me if I'd had a good day at school. I said that I had and then my dad showed me a phone bill.

'You've been doing a lot of texting,' he said,

'Huh?'

'The phone bill is huge,' explained my mum.

'Oh – right,' I replied, calming down.

My phone is on the same contract as my parents and I have a monthly limit that I'm not supposed to go over.

'*I'm* not going to pay for your excessive phone use,' said my dad, only he didn't seem that angry. In fact he seemed like he was trying not to laugh or something.

'No matter *how* much you text Jit,' said my mum. 'That's who it is, isn't it?'

'Yeah,' I said.

'But you see him all day, everyday at school,' added my dad. 'How much can you possibly have to talk about?'

I grinned at him. 'It's a teenage thing,' I said. 'You wouldn't understand, you old git . . .'

'Well the phone bill is a *money* thing. Maybe if you use *your* pocket money to pay for *your* overspend – you'll understand, you *young* git . . .' he replied.

'But dad . . .'

'No arguments, Suky,' said my mum. 'After this weekend your pocket money goes towards paying the bill . . . OK?'

I groaned.

'Whatever . . .'

'No letters today,' my dad told me.

'What?'

'No letters . . . you were expecting one from your pen pal?'

'Oh yeah . . . er . . . I'll e-mail her to find out what happened to it,' I told him.

'Funny girl,' said my mum. 'You'll be even worse when the baby is born . . . acting jealous and things . . .'

'Won't,' I said. 'I'm not a kid . . .'

My gran walked in with a cup of tea in her hands. She was spilling it everywhere.

'Careful, Mum,' my dad said to her in Punjabi.

'Oh go and poke out your own eyes,' she replied.

'Told!' I teased him, in English.

'And you can shut up too, you fat dog!' said my gran.

I looked at my mum and dad, who started to crease up with laughter.

'You horrible old gits . . .' I said angrily, stomping off to my room.

FOURTEEN

Justin and Andy were standing by the bus stop after school the next day, picking on a load of Year Sevens. I saw them from about fifty yards away and started to slow down. Grace, who was walking with me, asked me what was up, so I told her.

'Oh great! That's all we need after a whole afternoon of maths and science . . .' she moaned.

'What do we do?' I asked.

Grace shrugged. 'Nothing . . . we're going to get the bus and if they try and mess us about, I'll karate chop them – *yee-ah*!'

She kicked out her left leg and nearly went flying in the process.

'Oh, be serious, Grace . . .' I told her.

'Well we can't let them stop us from catching our bus – that would just be silly.'

'So, what do we do?' I asked.

'Simple – ignore them . . .' she replied.

That was easy to say. It proved impossible to do,

though. When we reached the bus stop, Andy was picking his nose and wiping what he found up his flared, hairy nostrils on a lad standing in front of him.

'*Yuk*!' said Grace, turning up her own nose. 'He's nasty.'

Andy did the same thing about three more times and then he saw us.

'Ah . . . it's the ugly twins,' he smirked.

Justin, who had another Year Seven by his ears, turned round and saw us too. He let the lad he was holding go and the poor kid ran off crying. Justin pulled out his mobile phone and videoed him running. Then he turned it towards me and Grace.

'So, you think you don't have to pay us?' he said to me, in a stupid posh accent.

'Get lost!' I replied, praying for the bus to turn up.

'Well, that's fine,' he told me. 'Splendid, in fact.'

'*Huh*?' I said, shocked.

'I admire your bravery in standing up to the school bully,' he continued.

Andy coughed.

'I'm sorry – did I say bully? I meant *bullies* . . .' corrected Justin.

I gave Grace a look that asked which drugs Justin was on. Then I looked back at him and he grinned at me, showing his manky, yellow teeth. They looked like they'd never been cleaned.

'After all,' he said, 'It takes *two* to tango . . .'

'I'm sorry?' I asked.

'No need to be sorry,' said Andy. 'Just think about it . . .' He was trying to copy Justin's terrible accent and doing even worse.

I looked at Grace again. She shrugged and put an index finger to her right temple, twirling it.

'*Loco* . . .' she whispered.

'Did you understand me?' asked Justin.

'Are you on drugs?' I asked.

Justin grinned again. 'Only you . . .' he smirked. 'Two to tango . . . remember that. Think about it . . . ta-ra!'

And with that he grabbed Andy by the shoulder and the two of them walked off.

'That was surreal,' said Grace.

'What does that mean?'

Grace shrugged. 'My mum says it all the time, when weird stuff happens . . .'

'Which is all the time in your house . . .'

'Yep!'

I watched the two bullies walking away and asked Grace if I was going mad. 'I think he just kind of asked me out,' I said, shocked at what my own voice was saying.

'*No*! Well, OK . . . maybe,' she replied.

'He told me that he was smiling because of me and then he kept saying it takes two to tango . . . and to *think* about it. Think about *what*?'

Grace shrugged again.

'But he could have meant *anything*,' she said.

'Yeah, but all the same . . .'

'It takes two *what* to tango, anyway?' she asked. 'Elephants? *Monkeys*?'

'That was so freaky,' I replied.

'I can see how it would be,' said Grace. 'Two elephants doing the tango. They'd need enormous dresses and reinforced high-heels too . . .'

The bus appeared in my line of vision just as she'd replied, saving me from even more weirdness.

Until I got home that is. Once again my parents were in the kitchen, snogging, when I walked in.

'Will you stop it!'? I shouted when I saw them. 'That's just *disgusting* . . .'

'Oh shut up you little witch!' replied my mum, as my dad turned purple and walked out of the kitchen.

'Oh my God!'

'*Well* . . . you're like a forty year old in a teenager's body. Why don't you take a chill pill?'

I raised an eyebrow.

'*OK* – snog all you like but whatever you do – *don't* say *that* in front of my friends – *ever OK*?' I told her.

'Say *what*?'

'*Chill Pill* – it's just *wrong* . . .'

My mum shook her head and sat down at the table.

'Imi rang for you . . .'

'When?' I asked.

'About five minutes ago . . .' she replied.

'What did he say?'

'Nothing much. Just to call him back when you got home . . .'

I wondered why he hadn't called me on my mobile.

'Must have been about the project,' I told her.

'You'll find out if you call him back,' she suggested, with added sarcasm.

'No need to be rude, is there?' I said, pulling my mobile out of my bag.

I found Imi's number and pressed the green dial button. Nothing happened. I hit cancel and then tried again. And again. And again. Still nothing.

'Bloody thing!' I shouted. 'It hasn't got a signal . . .'

My mum shook her head.

'I think you'll find it hasn't got a line,' she explained.

'What?'

'Your dad had it cut off temporarily . . .'

'That's not fair!' I shouted. 'I *need* this phone. What if I lose my number as well – that's just mean!'

'You won't lose the number. Your dad already checked that out. But you *will* pay back the money you owe. Maybe we'll change our minds after that.'

I sat down at the table.

'You were in on it too?' I asked.

'Yes. You owe twenty pounds on top of what your dad pays monthly. I mean – who were you calling – Santa Claus, in Lapland?'

I shrugged.

'Only Jit – and my other friends,' I said, quietly.

'Tough!' she replied, smiling slightly. The freak.

'I'd better use the landline,' I told her.

'Only if you're quick. And I mean super-quick . . .'

'*Whatever*!' I snapped, picking up the home phone and dialling.

Mrs Dhondy picked up the phone and I asked her if Imi was there.

'Oh, no, Suky. He's out with his dad. Won't be back until *very* late . . .'

'Can I leave him a message in that case?' I asked.

'Of course you can,' she told me.

'Can you ask him to call me as soon as he gets this message. Thank you . . .'

'You're welcome. Have fun at the seaside tomorrow,' said Mrs Dhondy before hanging up.

I turned to my mum.

'Did he say what he wanted?' I asked.

'*Who*?' she asked, being all vague.

'Imtiaz . . .'

'No – just something about calling him.'

'Nothing else?'

My mum shook her head.

'No. Now can you get a pen and a bit of paper please?' she asked.

'Why – you going to give me a *test*?' I replied.

'Uh-uh. We're going shopping,' she told me.

FIFTEEN

I opened the door to Jit the next morning and yawned at him.

'Hello to you, too,' he said, grinning.

'How can you be so *awake*?' I asked him. 'It's only seven am . . .'

'So?'

'*So* – you can't even make it to school for *nine* most mornings and here you are at seven am, looking all awake and *smiling* . . .'

Jit grinned. 'Maybe I'm excited about the trip?' he suggested.

'*Why?*'

'I've never been to the seaside before,' he admitted.

'Huh?'

'*Honest*. I've never seen the sea. Well I *have* but only in films and on the telly . . .'

I ushered him into the living room. 'You're lying . . . you must have seen it . . . not even when you were a little kid?'

He shook his head. 'I've never really been on holiday. My mum used to take me to London when I was younger – to go and look at the sights and that; but that's all,' he said.

'Oh,' I replied, not knowing what to say. It was too early in the morning anyway.

'I'm just going to get my stuff together,' I told him.

'Better get a coat too,' he told me. 'It ain't exactly warm out there.'

I groaned and left him in the room on his own for a few minutes. When I returned he was sitting on the sofa, pressed against one arm, as though he was trying to hide. The reason for this was that my gran was sitting almost on top of him, asking him questions in Punjabi.

'Gran – leave him alone.'

She looked at me and started to speak only I couldn't understand a word she was saying because she didn't have her teeth in. Jit actually looked scared but calmed down when she got up and walked out of the room.

'Having fun?' I teased.

'It's going to be like this all day,' he said.

'What was she saying?' I asked.

'I dunno. All I could see were her gums. Getting closer and closer. And she kept on farting – it was nasty . . .'

'Oh, she's harmless really,' I told him.

'*What*? She'd scare vampires, you get me.'

I laughed. 'She probably would too.'

I told him to come into the kitchen where my mum was making sandwiches and to pick out the ones he wanted so that he didn't end up with food he disliked. When my mum saw him she grinned broadly.

'Hello Jit!' she said.

'Hi . . .'

'What do you like then – in your sandwiches, I mean?'

'Er . . . I'm not that fussy really, Mrs . . .'

'Tina, please . . .' my mum told him.

'Tina.'

'I've got chicken and bacon in mayo, tuna mayo, ham, chicken, cheese and salad. And there's cold tandoori chicken pieces, barbecue wings, samosas and pakora too.'

Jit looked at the mountain of food in the kitchen.

'That's a *lot* of food,' he said.

'Oh didn't Suky tell you. Her uncle Mandeep and his family are coming too.'

Jit shot me a look and then smiled at my mum.

'Oh, yeah,' he said. 'I totally forgot . . .'

'Well – what do you *like* . . .?' continued my mum.

'Well *my* mum made me some too, but she didn't

make much, so can I have the chicken and bacon ones please?'

My mum smiled even wider.

'Growing boy like you needs to eat. Don't worry – I'll put a good selection together for you . . .'

I heard my dad come stomping down the stairs and went out into the hallway.

'You want me to go and fetch the lad?' he asked, swinging his keys in his hand.

'He's already here,' I told him.

'*Already*? He's a good lad, that Jit . . .'

'He's in the kitchen.'

My dad walked past me and into the kitchen. He saw all the food on the table, grabbed a pakora, coated it in mayonnaise and stuffed it into his gob. When he'd swallowed it, he asked Jit who'd dropped him off.

'My mum,' said Jit.

'And she didn't come and say *hello*?' asked my mum. 'You should have asked her in. I'm *dying* to meet her . . .'

Jit started going red so I stepped in.

'I'm sure you'll meet his parents soon enough,' I said. 'When they're good and ready. Not everyone is a forward as you two, you know.'

'But she could have just popped her head in the door and said hello,' suggested my mum.

'Next time,' said Jit. 'I'll ask her.'

My mum looked at my dad and then carried on making sandwiches, piles of them.

'You nearly done, Sweets?' asked my dad.

'Just about . . .' she replied.

'What time is Uncle Mandeep getting here?' I asked, hoping that we could off-load my gran on him.

'He's not,' replied my dad. 'Meeting us down there instead . . .'

'Oh,' I said.

Jit was eyeing the food so I asked him if he'd had any breakfast.

'Er . . . no – I don't normally eat breakfast . . .'

On hearing that my mum started fussing about how young people didn't look after themselves enough and she almost force-fed Jit a load of samosas and chicken. He didn't complain though, piling his way through it all. I don't know where he puts it – he's so skinny.

'Is Rita bringing food too?' asked my dad, talking about my aunt.

'I think so – but don't worry . . . it's going to be a long day and we'll get through it,' she replied, winking at him.

'You mean Dad will,' I said, laughing. 'Greedy fat boy really loves his food . . .'

'You cheeky cow!' he said, patting his belly. 'All bought and paid for, this . . .'

We were ready to go about fifteen minutes later and I asked Jit if he needed anything.

'I'm OK,' he said.

'I've got some books and stuff . . .'

He shrugged. 'I've got one book you'll love . . .'

'I ain't really into books and that,' he said.

'Trust me,' I told him. 'This one I'm on about is wicked. It's about normal kids . . . just like us.'

'Really?' he asked.

I nodded. 'It's by some guy that used to go to our school as well . . .'

'Nah!'

'Yeah . . . I've got it in one of my bags . . .'

I had three bags with me. A big one for my extra clothes and toiletries, a medium one to hold my books and magazines and stuff; and a smaller one, which was my carry bag. A girl's gotta be prepared. I pulled out the book and gave it to him. He started by looking at the colourful cover and then read the blurb on the back. By the time I had closed my bag he was on page one.

'See?'

'Sounds OK,' he told me. 'It's got swearing and sex on the first page, too!'

'It's cool – my mum bought it for me . . .'

Jit closed the book and told me he'd read some more on the journey.

'How long does it take?' he asked me.

'Two hours . . . maybe three. Depends on the traffic.'

My dad finished loading thc people carrier and told us to get in. Then he asked if I had seen my gran. I shrugged.

'Silly old goat,' he mumbled.

She emerged from her little granny annexe about five minutes later, still not wearing her teeth. When my dad asked her where they were, she fished them out of an old, battered handbag and showed them to him. He groaned and told her to put them in, which she did, and she only swore at him once. I smiled at Jit, as my gran got in. She sat in the middle row of seats and Jit and me sat in the back.

'Right!' said my dad, as my mum climbed aboard. 'Let's go!'

My gran called him a slimy, rancid toad, I think, and then she farted.

SIXTEEN

We stopped at a service station about two hours after leaving home. Jit had fallen asleep with the book that I'd given him open on his lap. I woke him up and asked him if he needed the loo.

'Wha'?'

'We've stopped at the services,' I said.

'Oh – right. Sorry I fell asleep,' he said, gathering himself together.

'No problem. You didn't miss much . . .'

'What were you doing?' he asked.

'Trying to ignore my gran and wondering why the roads are so boring.'

'Was she on one, yeah?'

'Just a bit,' I replied, getting out of the car.

Jit followed and stretched his arms, yawning. 'Where are we?' he asked.

'Dunno . . .'

'About an hour from the coast,' said my dad. 'I can smell the sea already . . .'

All *I* could smell was sewage works although that might have been my gran who had farted for the entire two hours. But it wasn't her fault. The poor woman had a wind problem. My dad asked us if we wanted drinks and then set off with my mum and my gran towards the shops. I told Jit I was going to the loo.

'I'll meet you outside,' he said, 'I need to go too.'

The service station was packed with people but none of them looked very happy. I suppose it was because it was such a horrible day, windy with little bits of rain. The clouds were a dark grey in the sky too. Not exactly the best day to go to the coast. Not that it had bothered my dad. When I'd bought it up on the journey, he'd just smiled and gone on about the bracing morning air and how the town we were going to had old smugglers' caves that you could visit.

'It's a great place,' he'd told me.

'Better be,' I'd replied.

Now, as I stood in the foyer, looking for the toilets, I prayed for a bit of sunshine. An old man walked past me and smiled.

'Cheer up love – it might never happen,' he said, all breezily.

I smiled back and wondered what might not happen and then I saw the sign for the ladies.

et back up with Jit five minutes later and we ked around the shops, going in and out, looking at things aimlessly.

'My mum gave me some spending money,' he told me. 'She never gives me money normally . . .'

'You won't need it,' I told him.

'Why?'

'My dad won't let you pay for anything . . .'

He shook his head. 'I'm not scrounging off your dad,' he told me. 'No way . . .'

I laughed. 'It's not scrounging, you fool. He's just got this Punjabi thing about taking guests anywhere. You're a guest so you don't pay. For anything . . .'

Jit thought about it for a moment as we stood in front of a magazine rack and then he grinned.

'What if I see a Ferrari that I want?'

I grinned back. 'Dickhead . . .'

'Well I'm gonna get my mum something and he's not paying for that,' he added.

Jit has had a hard life and I knew that his mum was poor. I was uncomfortable that my parents were so obviously well-off and I tried to think of something to say that wouldn't hurt his feelings. But in the end I was just honest.

'Don't tell him, then,' I suggested. 'Because he will pay for it if he sees you.'

Jit nodded and picked up a magazine with a semi-naked model on the front.

'Put that down – you dirty young man!' I shouted.

Jit looked around and saw people staring. He dropped the magazine and walked away, followed by me, laughing my head off.

'That wasn't fair,' he said.

'Oh – I was only kidding. You would have laughed if Grace had done it,' I replied.

'No I wouldn't . . .' he protested.

I smiled at him. 'Come on Jit. I reckon we know each other quite well now. You can admit that you fancy Grace . . . I won't tell.'

Jit shrugged. 'Even if I did,' he told me. 'She wouldn't go out with me. Me and her – we're too different . . .'

'Says who?' I asked.

'It's just the way it is,' he replied.

'She fancies you.'

'Huh?' He looked shocked.

'Of course she does . . . look at the way she's been funny about you and me seeing so much of each other . . .'

Jit thought for a moment. 'Did she *tell* you that she liked me?' he asked.

'Not in so many words. Me and Hannah just guessed . . .'

'So you don't really know then?'

'Jit! Everyone knows . . .'

He looked away, embarrassed.

'OK then,' I said to him. 'If she did like you – would you go out with her?'

'That ain't happenin',' he said, trying to deflect the question.

'But if it did . . . just pretend.'

'I dunno,' he replied. 'Probably, yeah . . .'

I had a brainwave.

'Do you want me to find out for you?' I asked.

'NO!' he said quickly.

'I won't make it obvious . . .'

'Just forget about it,' he told me, walking off towards the food court.

I followed him, only to find my parents looking worried.

'Your gran's gone walkabout,' said my mum.

'What?'

'We can't find her.'

'Well, she can't have got very far,' said Jit. 'It's not that big a place.'

My dad looked around and then suggested we split up to see if we could spot her.

'We'll meet back here in ten minutes and if you find her, don't let her out of your sight,' he said.

Me and Jit went to the car park first. It was packed with cars and coaches but we couldn't see her anywhere. We walked all the way round, approaching any old Indian women we could see, and there were quite a few, on a coach trip from Birmingham. It was just about to leave and we asked the driver if he had seen her. He shook his head and told us that he had counted his party back onto the coach.

'All here, innit,' he told us. 'Ain't got no extras . . .'

After asking the driver we went back inside and I searched the ladies whilst Jit looked in the shops. She wasn't anywhere to be seen. By the time we met up with my parents, my dad looked really worried.

'Where could she have gone?' he asked for about the fourth time.

In the end, after she'd been gone for over twenty minutes, we told the duty manager who put an announcement over the tannoy system.

'Would anyone who sees an old Asian lady looking lost please contact the nearest member of staff. She's wearing a traditional Asian outfit and has white hair. Five foot two with a limp and glasses.'

We were standing right next to the customer service desk when the manager made his announcement and I was well embarrassed. People were looking at us and pointing and stuff.

'I wish I was in the car . . .' I mumbled to Jit.

'Me too,' he whispered.

'She's always doing this,' moaned my dad. 'Senile old bat . . .'

'Oh leave her alone, Randeep,' snapped my mum. 'She can't help it . . .'

'Bloody can,' mumbled my dad. 'Does it on purpose . . .'

We stood and waited for another ten minutes and then the coach driver who we'd spoken to earlier turned up at the desk. My dad saw that he was Sikh and spoke to him in Punjabi, asking if he'd seen Gran. The coach driver smiled before he answered in his strong Anglo-Indian accent.

'The kids ask me earlier, innit. Said I didn't see her. But when I get back on motorway, one of the women in my party say she at back of coach, drinking tea and eating chapatti with other womens . . .'

My dad groaned.

'She very funny woman,' said the driver.

'Where is she?' asked my mum, in English.

'On the coach. Won't get off. Says that you don't feed her . . .'

'Oh my God!' I groaned. 'This is just too much!'

My dad shrugged.

'Best go get her then,' he said, thanking the driver as he led us out to the coach. My mum thanked the duty manager who was trying really hard not to burst into laughter.

When we got to the coach my gran was sitting at the back and my dad had to go on and coax her out. The other women, who my gran had been telling lies to, called my dad shameless and evil. As he helped Gran down the steps of the coach I heard one of the old women shout out.

'She wiped your backside for you and look what you do to her. No shame, you whoremonger!'

My gran started swearing at him too, and by the time he'd got her back into the car, he was sweating.

'Look at it this way,' my mum told him, smiling, 'things can't get any worse.'

My dad looked at my gran and then at Jit and me. 'Not for me they can't,' he said, mysteriously.

I shook my head. 'If you think you're going to lumber Jit and me with her . . .'

'We'll see,' he replied, chuckling to himself.

'Ooloo ka puttha!' spat my gran, which means 'you piece of owl poo.'

I smiled at Jit and shrugged, hoping he wouldn't hold my nutty family against me.

He just picked up his book and started reading.

SEVENTEEN

We arrived about an hour later and my dad found a place to park the car. Jit was really excited, asking me how close we were to the sea.

'Dunno,' I said.

My dad turned round and smiled at him.

'See those shops?' he asked.

'Yeah?'

'Just the other side of those . . .'

'Wicked!'

'Where are we meeting the rest of the family?' I asked.

'Dunno – Mandeep was supposed to call me when he got here. I'll wait until I hear from him.'

He shot my mum a look and I wondered whether he was as bothered by the size of our family party too. It would be like an army of Asians walking around.

We got out of the car after I'd put on a jacket and walked off towards the shops. There was a little walkway that led into a precinct full of little boutiques and gift shops.

My dad led the way, telling us that he'd been here loads as a teenager.

'Used to be a good market here. My uncle had a stall . . .'

The precinct led into a shopping centre where the shops were exactly the same as every other shopping centre in the country. My mum told my dad that she was tired.

'Can we sit down somewhere and get a coffee or something?'

'What?' shouted my gran, so loud that people stopped and looked at us.

'Tea?' my dad shouted at her.

'YES!' she said in an even louder voice.

I looked at Jit and then my mum. 'We're going for a walk,' I told her.

'OK but don't get lost . . .' she replied.

My dad snorted. 'You can't get lost around here – it's not big enough.'

'Well just be careful,' added my mum.

'We're going to have lunch at a little place called "Chathams",' said my dad. 'There's no point sitting in the car and eating the sandwiches. It'll be horrible. Besides they'll keep. Meet us at Chathams in an hour. You can't miss it . . . it's down along the seafront.'

'OK,' I replied, eager to get away.

Jit shrugged and told me that he wanted to go and see the sea. I looked at him like he was mad.

'The *sea*? Have you seen how *cold* it is out there?'

'But that's why I came,' he replied. 'I've never seen it . . .'

What I really wanted to do was hide somewhere warm, far away from my mad gran, but then I realised that Jit would have been really disappointed if he didn't get to go to the seafront. In the end I zipped up my jacket and nodded.

'OK then – but if I catch something – I'm going to beat you up . . .'

'Yeah, yeah,' grinned Jit. 'It's only a bit of rain, anyway.'

He marched down towards the exit and out into the rain. I waited a moment and then followed him. Outside, it was windy and grey and as we made our way down to the front, people walking in the opposite direction gave us funny looks.

'They think we're mad,' I pointed out to Jit.

'So? Who cares what they think?' he replied. He said something else too but his words got lost in a sudden gust of wind.

'Great!' I said.

We passed a few banks and some food places and then rounded a corner. In front of us, across a road, were the beach and then the sea. Jit looked at me, grinned like a little child and ran across. I waited until the road was clear and followed him. By the time I'd crossed the road he was on the sand, heading towards the sea.

'JIT!' I shouted at him, but he didn't hear me. He stood where he was and watched the waves crashing against the shore.

I looked up and down the beach and saw that it was almost deserted. There was a young woman walking a dog and an Asian man with a blonde woman standing under a shelter, talking. I walked carefully towards Jit and stood next to him.

'It's great, isn't it?' I said to him.

'Yeah,' he replied, lost in the view.

'You really haven't seen the sea before?'

'Nope.'

I put my hand on his shoulder and for once he didn't flinch or look away. Instead he looked at me and smiled.

'Have you ever swum in the sea?' he asked me.

'Yeah – lots . . .'

'What's it like?'

'Salty, wet, cold if it's around this country . . .'

'Oh . . .'

'Full of seaweed too . . .'

'You know people eat that, don't you?' he said.

'What, seaweed?'

He nodded as the young woman ran past us, chasing after her dog.

'Yeah, I saw it on some cookery show on the telly.'

'You're not as stupid as you pretend, are you?' I said, punching him on the arm.

'What do you want to do now?' he asked.

'I thought you wanted to look at the sea?'

'Done it,' he said, matter-of-factly. 'Besides it's not going anywhere, you get me?'

'I saw a little gift shop back in the little streets by the shopping centre. Maybe we can find your mum a present there?' I suggested.

'Yeah . . . let's do that.'

We walked back up to the road, past the shelter where the Asian man and his girlfriend were still sitting, talking to each other. The woman smiled as we passed and I smiled back. Then I looked at the man and thought that I recognised him. When we'd walked on about twenty metres I told Jit.

'I've seen that guy somewhere before,' I told him.

'What guy?'

'The Asian bloke back there . . .'

'Nah – he could be anyone . . .'

I shook my head.

'No – I've definitely seen his face – just can't remember where, that's all. It'll come to me . . .'

'Where's this shop then?' he asked, ignoring me.

'Down here,' I said, heading into a side street.

We didn't see anything that Jit wanted in the shop so instead we walked around some more, past amusement arcades and souvenir shops, half of them closed. I suppose it was quite late in the year for tourists. Not that I wanted the Union Jack bowler hats and flags or the topless postcards. Not to mention candy rock that would break the teeth on a shark and the nasty key rings. We also walked past the entrance to a cave tour, which was still open. The man at the entrance asked if we wanted to come in. I shook my head and said that we would come back after lunch.

'Fair enough,' he said, smiling broadly. 'Bring us a sandwich when you do!'

I looked at the time and told Jit that we needed to find Chathams.

'It's back along the road, I think,' I said.

'Back the way we came?' he asked.

'Yeah . . .'

'It's quite a small place, ain't it?'

'Very, although there's a load of roads past the seafront and the shops. And that big hill over there.'

Jit looked up and saw what I was on about.

'Is that a castle at the top?' he asked.

'What's left of it . . .'

'Castles, smugglers caves – it's great round here. We ain't got none of them things where we live . . .' he said.

'Yeah but we've got more people, better shops and lots of other stuff . . .' I pointed out. 'And besides it reminds me of them books I used to read when I was kid . . . The Famous something or other . . .'

Jit grinned. 'I used to read them too – they was lame . . .'

'Bet they were set in a place like this,' I said.

'Prob'ly,' he said, as we walked back past the shelter where the man I'd recognised had been sitting with his girlfriend. But they were gone so I didn't get another chance to look at him.

'He's gone,' I said out loud, with out meaning too.

'Who?' asked Jit.

'That bloke . . . the one I recognised,' I replied.

I didn't have long to wait to see him again. He was with

his girlfriend, sitting in the window of Chathams when we walked in. I smiled at him and he kind of smiled back, still wondering how I knew him. Then I saw my dad towards the back of the bar, where the room seemed to lead into another series of caves.

'They're in the back,' I said to Jit. 'Come on . . .'

I took one more look at the man but he didn't see me this time. He was too busy talking to his girlfriend.

My gran was her usual mad self whilst we were eating. First she took out her false teeth and put them down on the table next to her. Then, when the waitress came to take our orders, she started talking to her in Punjabi. The waitress was really polite and patient, even though she didn't have a clue what my gran was on about. She just smiled and said 'oh that's nice' when my gran finished speaking to her. My dad shrugged apologetically at the girl.

'Sorry about that,' he said to her.

'It's no problem,' said the waitress. 'Now what can I get for you?'

When the food arrived my gran dipped her finger in my mum's glass of water and started cleaning her false teeth.

'*Mum*!' said my dad in Punjabi, only to get a mouthful of abuse.

Jit stared at his food and tried not to crack up with laughter.

'So Jit,' said my dad. 'Tell me what your old man does again . . .'

'Huh?' asked Jit, looking up from his plate of fish and chips.

'Your dad – what does he do?'

I shot my dad a glare.

'He's already told you a million times,' I lied.

'I've forgotten,' replied my dad.

'He owns a load of fried chicken takeaways,' said Jit, remembering what he'd said last time.

The truth was that Jit didn't know what his dad did. He hadn't seen him since his parents had split up.

'Oh – only I don't know anyone with your family name who's got fried chicken shops in our city . . .'

'They're all in Birmingham and Coventry,' lied Jit.

I started feeling really bad for making him tell lies, especially as I was planning to tell my parents the truth anyway. So I jumped in.

'What does it matter what his dad does?' I asked. 'It's not a big deal . . .'

'I was only asking,' said my dad.

'Does that stupid skinny rat eat anything?' asked my gran in Punjabi.

Jit snorted with the strain of not laughing.

'I'm sorry Jit,' said my mum. 'For my husband *and* my mother-in-law.'

'It's OK,' said Jit. 'I don't really like talking about my family. I prefer to listen to other people . . .'

'I see,' replied my mum, looking at my dad.

'So, does our daughter bully you?' asked my dad.

'Dad!'

'Well, you are a bit of a madam . . .' he told me.

'I don't believe this,' I said.

Jit shrugged. 'She's a bit bossy at school and that,' he replied. 'And she loves to beat us at sprinting and other sports . . .'

'She doesn't make you do things against your will? Because she used to do that with one of her cousins – she even made him dress up in a skirt once,' continued my dad.

'I remember that,' said my mum. 'That was Rohan, wasn't it – poor lad,'

'He still hasn't got over it,' added my dad.

Jit looked at me and shook his head. 'No she doesn't make me do stuff like that,' he said.

My dad nodded,

'Interesting,' he said, 'only I've heard differently . . .'

The waitress came back before I could ask my dad

what he was on about. 'Your friends have arrived,' she told my parents.

'My dad looked over my shoulder to the front of the bar and grinned.

Assuming it was my uncle, I didn't bother turning around. It was Jit who saw them first.

'Oh *shit* . . .' he said.

'What's wrong?' I asked, before turning around and finding out for myself.

'Hi Suky,' said Imtiaz, half-smiling.

My mouth fell open and my heart sank. I gulped down air. Behind Imi were his parents, smiling at me.

EIGHTEEN

'Imtiaz told us everything,' said my dad, after I'd recovered from my shock.

'I tried to warn you,' Imi said to me. 'But you didn't return my call.'

I shot my mum a look.

'Don't look at *me* like that,' she said. 'I'm not the one who's been lying, am I?'

'But you let me and Jit carry on all day today and you knew,' I said.

My dad chuckled. So did Imi's.

'We wanted to see what else you'd come up with,' he told me.

'I can't believe that you kept it up for so long,' said Imi's mum.

'Shows a great deal of initiative,' said Mr Dhondy.

'And slyness,' added my dad.

'I'm so sorry,' I said, beginning to cry.

Jit just sat where he was, looking at anything but the people sitting around him. The waitress had moved us to a bigger table and we were the only people left in there. Even the owners were listening in on my shame. I looked at Jit and told *him* I was sorry too.

'Poor lad,' said my dad. 'You made him tell lies just so you could hide the truth . . .'

Jit looked up at the mention of his name. 'It wasn't all Suky's fault,' he replied. 'I went along with it and I didn't have to.'

My mum smiled at him. 'Yes, we know that. But that just makes you a good friend, as far as I'm concerned. Devious but a good friend . . .'

'And I didn't help either,' said Imi. 'I let Suky and Jit take all the risks and didn't do a thing. I could have told my parents . . .'

'Well you did eventually,' pointed out his mum.

'Yeah – only after those two idiots came round and grassed us all up!' he said.

What had happened was this. Justin and Andy had carried out their threat to tell the parents, only they had told Imi's parents and not mine. That had been on the Wednesday afternoon, after Andy had overheard Hannah and Grace talking. As we were all rushing to my house, thinking that Justin and Andy had gone there, the bullies were actually at Imi's house. Not that his mum had been too happy to see them.

'Very strange young men,' she told me. 'Sneering, ugly boys and one of them had the most unfortunate hair.'

Imi's parents had hidden what they knew from Imi because they wanted to speak to my parents first and, besides, they didn't know that Justin and Andy weren't just causing mischief. So Mrs Dhondy called my mum, who just happened to be sitting reading the phone bill at the time, and she checked the numbers I'd dialled the most. Between them they worked out that I had actually been on the phone to Imi and not Jit, as I'd claimed. Then between them and our fathers they'd come up with a devious little plan of their own. Which I was finding it hard to understand.

'But why all the trouble to bring us down *here* and tell us?' I asked. 'And lying about Uncle Mandeep coming too?'

My dad grinned at Imi's dad.

'You kids aren't the only ones who can plan things,' said Mr Dhondy.

'We thought we'd give you a little taste of your own medicine,' added my dad. 'Not nice, is it?'

He was right. I looked at Imi and tried to smile but it came out all wrong. Imi shrugged. He'd found out what was going on yesterday evening, which was why he'd called frantically. Not the stuff about the trip but the fact that his parents knew about me. He'd found his own phone bill, with my number underlined in red pen and a note next to it with my name on. But when he'd called, my mum had been first to the phone and the same thing had happened when I'd called back.

'So Imi was actually *in* when I rang back?' I asked his mum.

'Yes, sweetheart but I couldn't let you go and spoil our fun by talking to him, could I?' she said, shaking her head to make the point.

'And you were all in on it?'

This time my dad started laughing really hard. When I asked what was happening he said something really weird. He said 'Michael, too'. I looked at my mum.

'As in Michael *Parkhurst*? Grace's father . . .'

'Oh my God – did he know too?'

My dad held his sides and pointed to the door. I turned to see a smiling Mr Parkhurst with Grace, Dean and Hannah.

'Oh *great*! Bring the whole bloody school, why don't you?' I snapped.

'Oh don't be so silly, Suky. It could have been much worse. Besides your friends only found out on Friday night so they didn't get the chance to tell you . . .'

'On pain of a terrible and lingering death,' said Mr Parkhurst.

The adults said their hellos, except for my gran who just sat looking out of the window. Grace, Dean and Hannah were all wearing really long faces.

'Are you OK?' asked Grace.

'Yeah – why wouldn't I be? Sitting here with my shame exposed to the entire world . . . I'm peachy.'

'I was only asking,' she replied. 'How about you Jit?'

'I'm all right,' he told her. 'Feel a bit shitty though – because of all the lies and that.'

'Don't worry about that,' interrupted my dad. 'That was Suky's fault, not yours and besides I like you, whether you're going out with her or not. I was hoping we could still be friends . . .'

Jit looked at me and I nodded. 'I'd like that,' he told my dad.

'Well then,' said Grace's father, 'I guess we should all have a drink and chill out.'

'Dad!' said Grace.

'Yeah, Mr P,' teased Dean. 'Time we "chilled out", you get me?'

'I certainly do, bro . . .' winked Mr Parkhurst.

Hannah and Grace looked at each other and started giggling. I went over to Jit.

'I'm really sorry,' I said to him.

'Me too,' he replied.

'What have you got to be sorry for?'

'I could have just said no . . .' he pointed out.

I shook my head.

'No – this is down to me and Imi. No one else . . .'

'She's right,' added Imi. 'You've been a really good friend and I shouldn't have acted up over it, so I'm sorry too.'

Imi's mum coughed. 'Well if the apologies are going round then I suggest that you offer one to the rest of us too . . .' she said.

I looked at Imi, grinned and then shrugged.

We spent the rest of the day doing our own thing. Jit and the others went exploring whilst the parents just moved from café to bar to café again. I took Imi down to the beach and we sat in the shelter that I'd seen earlier. But not before we'd both been taken to one side by our parents.

'What else did your parents say to you?' he asked me.

'Nothing really – they were so cool about it . . .'

'Mine too,' he admitted.

'So basically we were worried about nothing at all?' I asked.

'Looks that way. I can't believe that they didn't get really angry though.'

I shrugged. 'Maybe they will when we get home?' I suggested.

'I can't see it,' said Imi. 'You heard the way they are with each other. My mum loves your mum . . .'

'Yeah and our dads are as stupid and silly and childish as each other . . .' I added.

'Exactly,' replied Imi.

I thought about what that meant. The fact that we wouldn't have to go around hiding any more and I smiled.

'You nuts or something?' asked Imi.

'*What*?'

'You're just staring out into the sea, smiling at nothing,' he said.

'I'm just thinking about school and not having to hide our relationship from anyone . . .'

'Yeah – that'll be a lot less stressful,' he admitted.

I turned to him and gave him a kiss, you know, a quiet moment, on our own? Fat chance. Somebody wolf-whistled and then cheered. I looked up and saw my friends, grinning back at me.

'Stop that this instant!' demanded Grace.

'Yeah,' said Dean. 'Come and check out the sights, man . . .'

'I wanna go in the caves,' demanded Hannah.

'Me too,' added Jit.

I looked at Imi and smiled. 'Oh come on then!' I said, standing up and joining my friends.

As we walked towards the smugglers' caves, Jit pointed something out to the rest of us. 'We've still got a problem with Justin and Andy,' he said.

'Oh yeah . . .' agreed Grace.

'Don't worry about that,' Dean said to us all, proudly.

'Why?' I asked. 'Have you come up with something?'

'Nah,' he replied. 'But I will. Them two bwoi can wait a while . . .'

'Yeah, I suppose they can,' I said to him.

'Still be there on Monday,' added Hannah.

The wind started to get up again and the rain clouds opened.

'Some day to come to the *bloody* seaside,' moaned Grace. 'I mean none of the *locals* are even outdoors, never mind walking along the coastal road. They're probably all watching us from their windows thinking "*look at those mental city folk*". And I'm not mental – I'm *not*!'

'Grace?' I said.

'Yes, sweetie?' she asked smiling.

'Will you shut up?'

'OK then . . .'

I grinned at Jit for what felt like the hundredth time.

'No more jugglin' then?' he said to me.

'I suppose not,' I replied. 'And I was having such fun, too!'

And I worked out who the Asian guy was too. He was *only* the *author* of the book that I'd given to Jit. Talk about coincidences. *Real* luck would have consisted of me recognising who he was straight away and having my book at hand. But then again, considering how easily I had gotten away with my deception, and the way my parents had reacted, I guess I'd used up my luck quota for, like, the Millennium or something. Oh well . . .